The Deaf Project
The first three chapters are engaging as we learn about an Italian family from New Jersey. The two teenage children, the grown and married daughter, and their mother, all face life altering changes together and their family bonds are inspiring. What I also love about this book so far is that I am learning about life in New Jersey and about being Italian, two things I couldn't even imagine before. I liked the inspirational quotes at the beginning of each chapter then I had to fan through the book to read the rest and behold, there are recipes and other goodies lurking in future chapters! I can't wait to read the next three chapters!

Hearing Elmo.com
"It's a Keeper."

SpeakupLibrarian.com
"My immediate reaction upon finishing the book was the recurring thought, 'It's been a privilege.'"

XpressiveHands.com
"I recommend this book for everyone, especially anyone taking deaf studies or learning ASL(American sign language). It is that good."

Welch's ASL Juice!
"A passionate heart she has for Deaf world!"

Candy Sweet Blog
"Turn a Deaf Ear points out a need for more true stories covering deaf/hearing relationships within the deaf culture."

Turn a Deaf Ear

By: Janet Fiore Horger
Linda Fiore Sanders

Grasshopper Christian Publishing
Dr. Zelma Frankhouser, Editor

Cover illustration created by:
Grasshopper Christian Publishing
www.consultant4nonprofits.com

Drawn by deaf student, Ethan Caudillo

Turn a Deaf Ear

By: Janet Fiore Horger
Linda Fiore Sanders

Printed in the United States of America

ISBN 13: 978-1461071891
ISBN 10: 1461071895

Copyright © April 2011 by Horger and Sanders

All rights reserved solely by the author. No part of this book may be reproduced in any form without the written permission of the author.

Contact the author to inquire about receiving copyright permission. Inquire at:

janhorger@yahoo.com
Send all inquiries to this e-mail address.

Turn a Deaf Ear

Table of Contents

Introduction vi

Dedications and Thanks viii

Prologue ix

Chapter 1, New Jersey 1

Chapter 2, East to West in Five Days 15

Chapter 3, California 41

Chapter 4, John 63

Chapter 5, John's Story 83

Chapter 6, Our New Life 91

Chapter 7, Mom 103

Chapter 8, A Chance Encounter 121

Chapter 9, Molly 127

Chapter 10, Heather 155

Chapter 11, Turn a Deaf Ear 177

Chapter 12, Splendida Famiglia 197

Epilogue 200

Website 203

Author Information 204

Coming Soon! 205

Photographer 206

ASL Sign Language Alphabet 207

Introduction

April 2010 I answered a knock at my front door. Standing there was a slim, golden-skinned, lovely lady with dark hair and a manila folder in her hand. She introduced herself as the mother of one of my neighbors. Her daughter, my neighbor, told her I had started a new book publishing business and that I was looking for stories. That was the beginning of a yearlong relationship that ended as a beautiful friendship.

Yes, I read the story that was in her manila folder and this book is the amazing finished product. Her story is about two sisters that take a true story and intertwine fascinating fiction to make it a pleasurable, tasty (lots of good food), and family-oriented reading. Their work presents examples of prejudice and the everyday struggles of deaf individuals. It centers on Linda's family and her extended silent family and Linda's life-changing marriage to a deaf man. The book takes twists and turns that keep the reader wondering what the next chapter will bring. Their story delivers a glimpse into the deaf world and gives the reader a snapshot of what it is like to live in a silent world. Enjoy *Turn a Deaf Ear* and their Splendida Famiglia!

Dr. Zelma J. Frankhouser, Editor
Turn a Deaf Ear
Grasshopper Christian Publishing
www.consultant4nonprofits.com

(The characters and the stories are fictional.)

Dedication and Thanks

John - for giving us this story.

Mom - a woman of strength. She came over from Italy to a new land, a new language and a new culture. Then she traveled across the United States to start a new life as a single mother. We continue to draw our strength from her today even though she is gone.

Jack - for his tireless support and patience

Zelma - for looking at a short story and saying "this needs to be a book!" For all your help in editing and publishing this book, and for the direction you led us to complete it. For all your hard work; for your faith and your love-thank you.

☙

Janet Fiore Horger
Linda Fiore Sanders

Prologue

My little sister wants to marry a deaf man!

I had no idea that something special
was about to happen to our family.

His name was John.

John wasn't handicapped; he was enriched.

He enriched our family and everyone that knew him.

It took courage for a young hearing girl to join the world of quiet but my sister jumped in with both feet. Taking on challenges, prejudice and criticism. We were just lucky enough to tag along for the journey.

Janet ଓ

When we met by chance, it wasn't at all as though our two worlds collided. It was as though they were completed.

Linda ଓ

Turn a Deaf Ear

*By
Jan Fiore Horger
and
Linda Fiore Sanders*

ଔ

"Once in a while,

Right in the middle of an ordinary life,

Love gives us a fairy tale."

Anonymous

ଔ

Chapter 1

New Jersey

I was content in New Jersey.

I lived in the same house all my life three blocks from the ocean. My best friend Maria lived two doors away. I was Tony Fiore's daughter, CeeCee's and Nick's younger sister, and mom's baby. Maria and I had just graduated from eighth grade and we were headed into the summer before our first year in high school.

I loved our beach town that lit up in the summer months with visitors from the city, and I also loved the boardwalk winters when everything was covered in snow.

"Hurry up Linda," Maria called.

"I'm coming," I answered as I lagged behind her lost in one of my daydreams.

"Keep your socks on, what's the hurry! Slow down and wait for me," I yelled back.

Maria retorted with, "I don't want to be waiting in a long line at Geli's because you are a slow poke. Ya' know there'll be a long line! Come on Linda! Quit your day dreaming!"

I put my arms down, stiff and straight by my side, and hurried my footsteps. I didn't want to give Maria the satisfaction of being right again about my daydreaming so I increased the length of my steps so I wouldn't be running when I caught up with her. Once beside Maria, I casually got in step with her.

Of course, Maria was right. She was always right when she said I was day dreaming again. Even though I loved my seaside home in New Jersey I often thought about what other towns and cities were like and how other people lived. I guess I really did have my head in the clouds as Maria said. Today was like any other day for Maria and me. We had a summer ritual.

Everyday we walked to the beach. First we would go to Geli's Gelato when they opened at eleven in the morning to get our favorite *Luscious Lemon Gelato*. Then we spent the entire day on the boardwalk or the beach. We tried S*umptuous Strawberry* and P*erfectly Peach* and we even tried *Mango Madness*. We both agreed that it was a good idea to try something new, but we always returned to our favorite *Luscious Lemon*.

Maria Longostina and I were friends since kindergarten when the Longostina family moved onto our block. They were Italian like our family. Maria had two older brothers and our families became immediate friends. Maria and I were inseparable. Mom said we were like twins even though we didn't look alike.

She was short and pudgy and wore glasses. Her hair was straight and cut short, not long and bushy like mine. She had long eyelashes and a beautiful smile. Even though my teeth were straight, I didn't smile a lot because I didn't like my smile.

We did everything together. We often moaned that our strict Italian parents would probably disown us if they knew we dreamed about being rich, sultry, movie stars who lived in Hollywood and had lots of handsome boyfriends.

We walked to and from school, did our homework together, ate at each other's houses, shared Photoplay magazines as we pretended we were movie stars. We went to church on Sundays together. We knew everything about each other, our thoughts, our dreams and our frustrations. Maria was one of the reasons I loved living in New Jersey – she was my best friend, forever!

I loved our old house, built on a tree-lined street with other old Victorian homes; all built during the 1850's. The houses were originally built as summer homes for the rich New York families who wanted to get out of the city during the summer. Mom told me that eventually as the years went by the rich vacated these summer homes and moved south to purchase the more modern, air-conditioned homes in Florida. Then other families like ours moved into the seaside homes and lived in them year round.

Nearly all the wood exteriors were painted gray or light blue with white trim. Most were single story with some that were two or three stories tall. Our house had three stories with wrap around porches on the east and south bottom two stories. When you walked into the first floor we had a large entry hall where creaky wooden stairs led to the second floor. The living room was on the first floor and was separated from the entry hall by *pocket doors* (doors that slide into the walls when opened). The living room windows faced the seashore where beautiful east-coast sunrises filled the room with the morning sun. The opposite wall, the west wall, had a fireplace that we never lit. Dad said the flue was broken and he never fixed it.

The room I liked most was on the first floor; it was the dining room, the largest room in the house. In the center was a large dining table with eight chairs. On the west wall was a China cabinet (a place for our good dishes, table cloths, good silverware and serving ware). Mom's piano sat at one end of the dining room, where mom displayed family photos. At the very end of the dining room was a large radiator with two large cast iron doors. When the doors were opened there was a shelf to keep food warm. This was called a warming oven; we learned the hard way not to touch it when it was hot.

The first floor also housed the kitchen. It was small with a gas stove, a big yellow-stained sink and a small wooden table with four chairs. There were cabinets for dishes but no doors on the cabinets. There was no dishwasher. Mom cooked every day but on Sundays dad would join her. They were both good cooks.

Every night mom served dinner at 6:30 p.m. sharp! That was when dad came home from his cleaning and tailor shop. On Sundays we ate at 2:00 p.m. in the afternoon. Many times Maria's entire family joined us for Sunday dinners, especially when dad made his homemade ravioli and Italian sausages. I loved when dad made homemade ravioli. He always made a big production of it. We all had to be involved.

First dad mixed up the dough with flour, eggs and water. Then he kneaded it and let it rest for a while. Then he rolled out the ravioli strips. Next it was my job to mix up the ricotta, eggs, parsley and grated Italian cheese.

> Dad would taste it and say, "I think it needs a little salt."

Dad would then place a teaspoon full of the ricotta mixture exactly two inches apart. It would take three of us to fold over the dough to touch the opposite edge. He cupped his hands around each *pillow* of filled dough and cut each one apart. The final part was the assembly line. They were the *forkers*. Usually Nick (my older brother) and Maria liked to do that. I always suspected Maria had a crush on Nick but she never admitted it to me.

The job of the *forker* was to take the tip of the fork and press the three edges of the raviolis to keep the folded dough from separating during cooking. The best part was eating what we made together as friends and family. Each bite tasted extra special because we all had a hand in creating it from scratch.

The dinner table was always loud with everyone talking at once, eating and passing food. Dad always had a story to tell from the old days and I loved to listen to them told over and over again; mom would roll her eyes each time a story became a bit more exaggerated. As I look back, our New Jersey home was a place of many happy memories especially around mealtimes.

Upstairs there were four bedrooms and it held the only modern bathroom in the house. It was added after the house was built because the pipes were run outside of the house. There was a bedroom for mom and dad, one each for my brother and me, and one bedroom that used to be CeeCee's now used for company. My bedroom was in the corner and it had windows looking out two different directions. My room and every bedroom was covered with flowered wallpaper. The hardwood bedroom floors were adorned with brightly colored large throw rugs and the wooden floors creaked every time you walked on them.

Maria and I spent a lot of time in my room. One window opened up to the upstairs porch where we could see the ocean. When we were little we played with our dolls on that porch. We had no air conditioning and during the hot summers when we were older, we slept on the porch with our pillows and blankets as our beds. The porch was the perfect place to catch the cool evening breezes from the Atlantic Ocean.

We read the home decor magazines at the local drug store, then rushed home and tried to duplicate the pictures in the magazines. Maria and I often attempted to redecorate my bedroom. We tried to repeat the same decor for her bedroom that was just two houses down from my home. Many times our efforts were utter failures, but our parents were very patient with us as we struggled to become fashionable decorators. One time we decided to make my room into a circus theme. We pitched a tent made out of sheets over my bed and used stuffed animals as the zoo. Our tent was not solidly tethered and it fell in on both of us the first time we sat on the bed, and we rolled over in laughter.

Our house had a third floor but I never ventured up there by myself. Mother said it used to be the maid's quarters. The walls were white and void of the pretty flowery wallpaper that adorned our bedroom walls. We didn't have a maid, butler, housekeeper, or baby sitter, so mom used the third floor to store extra family things. Sometimes, late in the night I thought I heard footsteps in the maid's room. I fantasized that a ghost was wandering around. I would pull the covers over my head so I could hide from the ghost if it came into my room. Mom soothed my fears by telling me the noises were just the normal sounds of an old-wooden house settling as the wood cracked and bent.

Our town was small. We had one movie house, a diner, one grocery market, and one general store (a hardware store) and a mercantile that sold clothes, linens and books. We had a bank and a small library that was housed with the post office. We also had a Woolworth's five and dime. We had a Rexall Drug Store, with an orange and blue vertical sign with counters for quick lunches, ice cream, and a flavored soda. It doubled as a place to eat, read the latest magazines, and visit with friends. The pharmacist, Mr. Sharpton, was always very friendly and helpful to those who could not afford to go to a doctor. Next to the drug store was our hometown bakery where we could buy Charlotte Rousse pastries and Streusel Coffee Cake buns, yummy!

The school I went to (as well as CeeCee and Nick) was a single building that housed kindergarten through high school. It was a big three-story brick building. The little kids had classrooms on the first floor, the pre-teens were on the second floor, and the high school was on the third floor. Maria and I were anxious to finally be in high school on the third floor. It was a status symbol for us.

The best part of our town was the boardwalk that opened during the summer with all types of rides. The second best part was the beach. Maria and I would people watch on the boardwalk during the summer months when our town came alive. It was a drastic change from the cold, dark, and windy winters when all the shops and rides were shut down. Our boardwalk and beach were crowded with vacationing city families. It was hot and humid in the city and the breezes of the Atlantic Ocean lured them to our shores. They came for the games and rides and vendors selling flashy, cheap plastic jewelry, flowery scarves, pink cotton candy, salt water taffy and little souvenirs made of seashells and, of course, the warm water and beaches.

Not only did strangers flock to our beach, but also our relatives loved to come to our house from Newark. They came because our house had extra rooms and was a short walk to the summer fun. Summers were filled with relatives because mom and dad came from large families. It seemed that as soon as school was out, our house was filled with a different bunch of relatives every weekend.

These were fun times and mom and dad made them extra special by serving big Italian meals in our dining room. The aroma of their cooking melted into every part of our house. The smell of tasty Italian spices and sausages, tangy sauces, and garlic bread escaped from our open windows and enticed us kids to rush home just in time for dinner to be served. I usually made it home in time to wash off the sand and grit from the day on the beach and run downstairs just in time for grace to be said.

Yes, I was content in New Jersey even though Maria and I were teased unmercifully for our Italian heritage. There was a group of unruly, rude and obnoxious boys that tormented Maria and I when they spied us walking together. They always tried to block our way and spewed unkind remarks at us. They never missed a chance to harass us as we walked to school.

> "Hey Guinea! How does an Italian machine gun sound? Wop! Wop! Wop!"

There it was, my very first taste of bullying and prejudice and I didn't even know what the word prejudice meant. We cringed in fear and our faces burned with embarrassment. Maria would grab my hand and give me the *don't back down and be a sissy look,* and I would stiffen my back, hold my school books tighter to my chest, look down and walk by quickly, muttering under my breath, jerks! It was during those times I wished I knew how to speak fluent Italian so I could rebut their taunting in a language they couldn't understand. Unfortunately, mom and dad refused to teach Italian to us. Mom and dad would tell us,

> "We are in America now we speak English only!"

At home, I would hear them talking in hushed tones to each other in Italian and I tried to listen carefully so I could learn their secret language. Little did I know that I would eventually learn another secret language!

I was truly content in New Jersey, but unfortunately that was all going to change. Three weeks after I graduated from grammar school and Nick graduated from high school mom sat us down and told us that after twenty eight years of marriage dad wanted a divorce because he was in love with another woman. Dad was leaving and not coming back and we were moving to California!

Mom told us we were going to start a new life without dad. We were moving to California to be near my sister Cecilia (CeeCee) and her husband Fred and their two children Kerri and Freddie Jr. Nick and I sat in silence as mom gave us the details. I guess we were both in shock and couldn't think of anything to say. We didn't even object. Maybe it was because mom was choking back tears while telling us and we didn't want her to be even more upset. That night I tossed in my sleep. I kept thinking, our dad was leaving, had he already left? Was it my fault? Please, let this be a bad dream and when I wake up everything will be normal.

Why didn't I see this coming? I used to hear them arguing once in a while, but I thought that was normal. How was I going to leave the only home I knew to go so far away? How was I going to tell Maria, my very best friend in the world that we wouldn't go to high school together and wouldn't spend the entire summer at the beach?

"A part of us remains
Wherever we have been."

Anonymous

Chapter 2

East to West in Five Days

I was numb with fear.

All that night my head swam with questions about this horrific change in my life. Mom told Nick and I we were leaving in two short weeks! Not a lot of time to spend with Maria, no time to get used to anything at all - I was numb with fear. Boom – just like that, we weren't a family anymore and I didn't have a chance to protest; it was a done deal. It wasn't fair, not fair at all! Dad turned my life upside down and I was ripped and torn inside and my heart was bleeding from anger and sorrow. I couldn't accept that my home in New Jersey and my best friend Maria were both gone. How could he do this to us, to me? When I finally fully awakened from my troubling thoughts my eyes had darker circles than normal. My stomach was so tied in knots I couldn't eat the eggs mom made for us. I just stared at my plate, in a state of confusion and sheer shock. Nick, on the other hand, didn't have trouble gobbling his breakfast down, so I gave him what I didn't eat.

That morning Nick was full of talk about surfing and hanging out at the beach. He talked about California girls and the California sun as if his lifetime dream was to live in California. I couldn't join in the conversation, all I could think was how awful it was to leave Maria and being stuck in an unfamiliar place. I just knew in my heart that I would be out of place and everyone would laugh at the skinny Italian girl with the funny New Jersey accent and the thick brown hair that seemed to never want to keep a style. Ugh! I was going to be in a new high school without Maria. I couldn't imagine my life without her. We always leaned on each other. I didn't make friends easily because I was so shy and self-conscious about my looks, but I didn't care because I had Maria, we had each other. I was frozen by fear and anxiety. The days passed quickly and it was time to pack and leave.

Day One

With a heavy heart I helped pack the Rambler station wagon. Mom said not to worry because she had enough money for us to make the long trip. My brother said we would be driving almost three thousand miles and that if we drive all day and rest at night we should get to CeeCee's place on the fifth day. He said it would be a great adventure because we would go places and see things that were new and exciting like Disneyland! Believe me, I didn't share his enthusiasm.

Newness was not what I longed for. I wanted security, friends, and everything I loved about New Jersey. Later that morning we carried our suitcases and boxes with totally opposite attitudes. Nick ran and jumped while he sang songs about California sunshine. Every movement I made was out of numbness. Mom said I looked like a turtle with my head stuck in the shell. Somehow, I just couldn't rush the last minutes I had to spend at home. I thought and prayed, please Lord, make mom change her mind because I knew this move would be the death of me and saying goodbye to my best friend was something I dreaded.

Saying goodbye to Maria was worse than I imagined. We hugged until our arms hurt and we cried until our eyes were almost swollen shut. I just couldn't let go. I wanted to hold onto both Maria and my wonderful life in New Jersey. We promised we would write every day. Our secret plan was that I would graduate high school, get a job and an apartment and Maria would join me when she graduated. She would come to California and we would share an apartment together and meet lots of movie stars and become glamorous.

We promised to never tell anyone else about our plan because it was what made our parting tolerable. We had a special secret to share and it would live in our hearts and keep us together. Maria didn't go home, she stayed all morning and helped me pack and load the Rambler. Even with Maria helping, it took all morning to pack suitcases in the back and up on the Rambler's roof rack. We put an ice chest full of food in the back. With the Rambler loaded, filled, and tires getting lower because of the weight - we started our east to west journey.

> Mom said, "At least we got a decent car and the tires are brand new!"

She didn't expect too many problems with the car, but I could see in her eyes a hint of sadness at leaving her home and family. I thought it very strange that none of our relatives came to see us off. The only person waiving to us as we left was Maria. That day we started our journey in total silence and me with swollen eyes and craning my neck to wave goodbye to Maria and my home until they were out of sight. Then I turned facing the highway ahead of us and slumped down in my seat with my head in my hands. Nick turned to face me.

> "Linda, don't be such a cry baby! Just think, in five days we will be in California and close to the beach. It won't be a lot different than New Jersey because we will still have the ocean and the beach. Come on, dry up those tears and think about seeing CeeCee again!"

Mom said, "Nick, let her cry it out. She has almost five days to get used to the change. Just be patient with her and let her deal with it in her own way."

Nick shrugged his shoulders, "All right. I guess you are right mom, but I hate it when she blubbers like that. Why can't girls be more like guys and think of life as an adventure?"

Mom replied, "Because they aren't guys, they are girls!"

Nick said, "Whatever. I guess I will never get it."

Nick's attempt to cheer me up failed. The tears burned as they filled my swollen eyes. Nothing more was said about my crying and I eventually ran out of tears. I finally sat up and tried to see where we were. Then it happened. When we crossed the New Jersey state line, mom had to pull over because she started crying. She knew her marriage of twenty-eight years was over. She left behind sisters and brothers and many years of memories in New Jersey. My heart went out to her as she sobbed and sobbed. Nick and I didn't know what to do. I leaned over from the back seat and put my arms around mom. I told her everything would be okay. Right there was the beginning of our close relationship, one that would last a lifetime.

At that moment, she became more important to me than my own sorrow. Nick held his head down and with a deep, choked up voice agreed with me. Mom had been so strong and confident before we started the trip; her breakdown was a surprise to us. I guess mom's crying was just what she needed, because when she stopped she blew her nose, squared her shoulders, started the Rambler and started driving. As I remember, she never cried another time during the trip, even when things got really tough and scary.

That first day, Nick told mom not to worry because he was the man now and he would take care of both of us. Nick had just graduated high school, was seventeen and one-half years old, and in his mind, he was truly grown up. Nick sat in the front with mom and I sat in the back. At first I was upset that I didn't get a turn in the front but then I adopted the back seat as my new home. I had a pillow and a blanket and could stretch out to sleep, anytime I wanted. I had a notebook to write down my thoughts and letters to Maria.

As we drove I could look out the window at all the new sights and do what Maria said I do best, daydream. During the hours and days in the backseat I was able to daydream, write, look at the new sights, and imagine what California looked like. My days began to be filled with visions of hanging out at the beach with my new friends and with a really cool tan. I even imagined that I might bleach a few strands of my hair and put it in braids with beads threaded throughout the braids. (I also imagined that mom would not approve.) Mom never shared with us her dreams of our new life in California. Nick did.

He talked a lot about the California girls with their blond hair and suntanned bodies. He often pretended at night in the motel rooms to be surfing and riding the waves as he stood on the bed. I would laugh and tease him because he didn't own a surfboard and had never been on one, before. I know it was silly, but it kept us from getting too bored with our trip. As for me, deep inside I was still grieving for my loss of New Jersey and Maria.

Those days we didn't have cell phones and pay phones were few and far between. Sometimes mom would stop and make a call to CeeCee or a relative in New Jersey. She did this to let them know we were okay and were still determined to make it to the west coast. I don't remember mom ever calling dad to let him know we were safe. I often wonder what dad was thinking and if he worried about his kids who were so far from home.

If he ever was worried, he never told us when we saw him many years later; when we were adults. Dad didn't come to see us off and he didn't write us letters while we were in California. Many times during the trip I saw neat postcards and I wanted to buy one and send it to dad. But I didn't because I didn't know his new address and I was certainly not going to ask mom for it. Mom was hurt enough by what dad did and I knew if I asked her she would be reminded of dad's infidelity. I thought mom had enough worry and stress in her life as we made our east to west journey; reminding her of dad and his new girlfriend wasn't fair to mom. I was hoping, and I think mom was too, that dad would change his mind after a while and come after us.

During our trip, Nick did most of the driving. Mom drove when he got tired and let him sleep. I was only fourteen years old, so I was delegated to making the sandwiches and supplying drinks when Nick and mom were thirsty. If we all got tired, then we decided we would pull off the road and take a nap. As mom or Nick drove, I watched things whiz by. Since I had never seen any of this country before, I often wished we could stop and see things like, *The World's Largest Dinosaur Egg*. The big, flashy signs fascinated me and my curiosity would conjure images of what the signs advertised. I wrote to Maria and asked how big was a regular dinosaur egg? Then I would try to vision how big it was. Was it bigger than a TV or bigger than a car? Was it white, black, or brown? Where was it found and what was it in – rock, mud, a tree, or tar? Was there a baby dinosaur in the egg? How was it preserved for millions of years? Was it cracked or all in one piece? I had lots of questions and had only my imagination for the answers because we kept driving and kept whizzing by the fascinating signs.

As we drove, we took Route 80 out of New Jersey and dropped down to Highway 40 through the southern part of the country. The first day we drove until dusk. Mom did not want us to drive at night. She wanted her family to be safe and tucked in before sundown. The first night we spent in Wheeling, West Virginia. We found a cheap motel and mom and I slept in the bed while Nick slept on blankets on the floor.

Day Two

The next day, we arrived in Memphis, Tennessee and got out to stretch our legs and get some food. I wandered around, trying to take in all the different sights and smells of the hot, humid southern environment. I was thirsty, so I took a drink out of the water fountain near the bathroom. An older white woman grabbed me by the shoulders and pulled me away.

> She whispered in my ear, "You don't want to do that child, that's black."

I had no idea what she was telling me, so I looked down at the fountain.

> I whispered back, "You mean the water is black?"

She smiled a funny smile, it was more like an - *Are you stupid or what*, smile. She pointed to a fountain that looked exactly the same as the one from which I was trying to get a drink

>She said, "You aren't from these parts, are you? Don't you northerners know anything? That water is for blacks folks, only. We got water fountains for the whites, down here so we don't have to share with the blacks. The white fountain is over there."

I politely thanked her and walked to the *white only* water fountain, got my drink and walked away. I made a mental note to tell mom about this funny town that separated the drinking fountains by white and black. Of course, I could not connect with the southern prejudice against blacks, because I never experienced it in New Jersey. Prejudice because of skin color was something new to me and after this experience I knew it was something that I didn't like. It made me feel uneasy and uncomfortable. It was an eerie feeling that I hoped would not be repeated in California.

After our break to stretch our legs and walk around, we got back in our (now hot) Rambler and continued our trip through the southern states. The landscape was green and there were a lot of trees. We would see few cities and many farms and ranches. The heat was burning and the humidity made it hard to breathe. To keep out of the wretched weather, we tried to reduce stopping to just gas or food.

I soon got bored so we thought of a game to play to keep Nick, mom, and me from going to sleep as we traveled. We decided to look for New Jersey license plates as we counted down the miles. I can't recall if we saw any or if I eventually dozed off and slept. I don't remember checking into a motel. Mom and Nick probably carried me to our room because all I remember is waking up very early the next morning as mom shook me awake. I remember we left very early and it was already hot and the air was still and sticky.

Day Three

I think the hot weather made me sleepy because I think I slept through most of day three because I don't remember much about it. Soon we were in eastern Oklahoma. The only thing I knew about Oklahoma were stories of Indians and tornadoes. Suddenly the road ahead turned an ugly, threatening black. Nick said there was a storm coming. Then, something hit the windshield with a big splat, then another and another. Nick turned on the windshield wipers and smeared dead grasshoppers on the windshield. Mom told Nick to pull over and turn off the windshield wipers. I heard so many splats hitting the car that I put my hands over my ears. I looked to my right and saw hundreds of grasshoppers clinging to the windows; they were all over the car. I screamed. Mom put her hand on my shoulder and told me to shut my eyes. She said that soon they would fly over.

The grasshoppers kept coming and our car got so dark inside I couldn't tell if it was day or night. I could still hear their awful buzzing noise and the thump as they landed and hit our car. I thought the grasshoppers were in our car because I couldn't see anything. I tried to brush them off my skin, but nothing was there. I began to cry and moan. Mom climbed into the backseat and held me in her arms until the blackness and the deafening noise of the grasshoppers stopped. When the car filled with light again, I opened my eyes and looked at Nick. He appeared to be frozen with his hands still on the steering wheel of the car. I don't think Nick said one word during the ordeal. Then, he began to shake and sweat. Without the car being on, the air conditioner was turned off and the car was stifling hot.

> Mom yelled at Nick, "Nick-take a deep breath! Start the car again! Turn on the air; the car is too hot and you are getting sick!"

Like a robot, Nick did exactly as mom said. Soon cool air was filling the car and Nick began to calm down. Mom told Nick to slide over and she would drive. She said the road may be slippery from dead bugs and the slippery road was too dangerous for Nick to try and navigate. Mom decided to wipe off the windshield before we started. She opened her door and grasshoppers were crawling all over the pavement. I gave her a towel and cup of water and she washed off one side of the windshield. When she opened the door to get in, a grasshopper jumped in the car. I screamed, again. Mom calmly took the wet towel and picked up the grasshopper and threw it out the door. As she drove off we could hear the snap and crack of crushed grasshoppers as she drove over them. Occasionally, a lone grasshopper hit our windshield, but mom kept on driving and eventually the critter would fly away.

As we drove through Oklahoma we could see the terrible damage the grasshoppers did to the trees and bushes alongside the road. The wheat fields were uneven due to the grasshoppers eating the crop. Sometimes I saw farmers walking the wheat fields as if to assess the damage. It looked to me as if the wheat was ready to be harvested, and now the crop was ruined. I thought to myself that being a wheat farmer in Oklahoma must be a risky job. I felt sorry for them. But most of all, I was glad the nightmare was over and I knew Nick and mom were glad too.

Mom said, "Now I know how the Egyptians felt in the Old Testament when they were tormented with the locust plague. You know grasshoppers are sometimes called locusts and they eat everything in their way when they swarm. It is a terrible thing to see and now I know it is a terrible thing to live through."

Nick and I both shook our heads in agreement. The grasshopper nightmare kept me from sleeping or daydreaming. I kept on the lookout for more black clouds all the way through Oklahoma. I was glad we only had to stop for gas one time in Oklahoma, and that was in a big city. While getting gas, all of us pulled dead grasshoppers off the car and off the front of the car. There were so many bugs on the front of the car that they almost completely covered the lights, grill, bumper, and the radiator. A worker at the gas station got a water hose and sprayed the outside of the car. He sprayed off our radiator and even the engine until the bugs were gone. He said many other travelers came into his station with the same problem,.

"A plugged up radiator would be pretty fearsome for travelers during this hot summer. It wouldn't have been long until your car would overheat and you would be stuck between here and Texas. I sure would hate to know that I didn't do something to help you travelers," he said with his thick southern drawl.

We were happy he helped us because we never thought of opening the hood and looking inside to see what damage was done. When we drove off, he was washing the bugs into a big hole and waving to us with a big, toothless smile.

> Mom said, "What a nice man. I wonder if all Oklahoma folks are all as nice as he?"

It was dark by now and mom let Nick drive through the rest of Oklahoma and through the panhandle of Texas. Nick drove us to a town called Amarillo. Mom said Amarillo means yellow in Spanish. We stopped in Amarillo and ate and walked around. The town looked old and some of the people looked like Indians. It was dusty and the buildings were made of brick and looked really old. We slept in our car because we couldn't find a place to spend the entire night. Even though Amarillo was hot during the day, the nights were cooler and a light breeze was blowing, so our rest was cool and pleasant. The next morning we drove to a gas station and washed up and started the drive to New Mexico.

Day Four

The fourth day of travel took us through New Mexico, which was hot and barren. Only a few Indian stores dotted the highway. Sometimes there was a gas station that also had a small coffee shop. We stopped on occasion and ordered a cold soft drink. Since my experience with the black water fountain, I learned to look around before getting a drink or going to the restroom. I didn't see any signs about blacks or whites, however, the yellow water that spouted from the drinking fountain looked awful. I decided not to get a drink of fountain water in New Mexico! The absence of the black only and white only signs put me more at ease. Even though the desert was barren and it was extremely hot, I felt more at ease traveling through New Mexico than I did in the southern states. It seemed as if the drive through New Mexico was terribly long. I think I drifted off to sleep a few times because soon I saw a sign that said we were entering Arizona.

We spent our last night in Flagstaff, Arizona and planned to cross over into California at Needles the next day. The night we stayed in Flagstaff, mom put a chair under the door knob so no one could break in without our hearing them. This was the first time I didn't feel safe on the road (other than the grasshopper storm). I didn't sleep well because I kept listening for an intruder. The bathtubs in the motel were dirty and stained with rust. We decided it was best to take a sponge bath. We promised ourselves a reward when we got to CeeCee's; a long-hot shower in a clean bathroom with soft towels and lots of good-smelling bath soap.
We had been on the road for over four long days and nights. The Rambler performed well, but all three of us were tired of being cooped up in it

and we were anxious to get to our California family. Most of all, I wanted to sit down at a table and eat a home-cooked meal. I was tired of sandwiches and gas stations. I wanted a good night's sleep in a bed and one of CeeCee's delicious Italian meals. Mom got us up before dawn. She wanted to get to CeeCee's by dinnertime, and she said we still had a long way to go before we made Los Angeles. Groggy, stiff, and bone tired of motels and the back seat of the car, it didn't take much to motive us to get up and get in the Rambler.

Day Five

Day five, we crossed into California. We had to go through an inspection station. The people at the station wanted to know if we were bringing fruit or plants into California. I thought - *Yeah, right. If we had any fresh fruit we would have already eaten it or it would be rotten by the time we reached the California border.* All three of us were tired but we were so excited to be in California we all let out a yell for joy as we left the inspection station. It was a good feeling to be this close to relatives again.

Mom told us to look out for a post office or a store that might have a pay phone so she could call CeeCee. Nick was the first to spy a pay phone. He pointed to the run-down storefront and mom stopped and parked the car to call CeeCee. Nick and I stayed in the car for a little while; we soon jumped out because it was stifling hot in the car. The three of us walked into the store and mom asked the man standing at the cash register if they had a public bathroom. He said no, but the gas station up the street was open, but you had to ask the gas station attendant for a key to open the door.

All I can say about the bathroom was it was just as dusty and dirty as the town. I thought, I wasn't looking forward to returning to this place called Needles anytime in the near future and the sooner we left, the better. Mom put some gas in the Rambler and we were on the road again; soon Needles was just a dot in our back window. I gladly waived goodbye to Needles and was happy to be headed toward our new home. Mom said CeeCee was anxiously waiting for our arrival with spaghetti and meatballs planned for a big welcoming dinner. The mention of home cooking, especially Italian food, made my stomach growl. The landscape was different in California. There were palm trees everywhere and the mountains were beautiful. Mom noticed that the weather was drier. The roads were wide and there were no toll booths on the freeways. I craned my neck to look for signs of Disneyland, but none were to be seen.

Suddenly, our car began to bump up and down and we heard a flop, flop, and a small cloud of dust popped up from the front of the car. Mom was driving, thank goodness, because Nick wouldn't have known how to handle the car. Mom knew exactly what to do. She didn't brake or turn the wheel – she let off the gas and let the car slow down. When the car slowed down, mom carefully turned the wheel and guided the car to the dirt shoulder of the road. Mom gently pumped the brakes - thump, thump, then stop. The other cars behind us saw the problem and waved as they passed us. I saw the passengers point to our front, left wheel. Mom turned to us bravely with a quiver in her voice and said,

> "Well, kids. We are almost there and the Rambler gets a flat tire. Don't get out of the car because the traffic is pretty heavy on this highway. I know we have a spare in the back; the problem is we got tons of stuff packed in this car and jacking it up will take a Goliath of a man!"

Just then, as if in answer to prayer, a big truck pulled off the road ahead of us. We couldn't see very well through the thick cloud of dust and gravel that the truck stirred up, but we could hear his air brakes take hold and stop the big rig. A husky, bearded man stepped out of the cab and walked to the car. I thought, yep – this is our Goliath! Mom rolled down her window and the big man bent down to talk to mom. He said,
> "I see you folks are from New Jersey and you got a flat tire. One of the truckers ahead of me radioed that you were stuck here on the side of the road with kids in

the car. Well, I am a married man with kids of my own and I thought I should stop and give you and your kids a hand. Ma'am, do you have a spare tire? You and the kids can sit in my truck cab while I fix your tire. I own my truck and I am an independent hauler, so go right ahead and sit in the truck and just relax. I will have your car fixed in no time."

Mom looked at the man and started to tear up. The big man pulled off his hat and said,

"It ain't no reason to cry, you are in good hands."

He opened the car door for mom and escorted her to the cab and we jumped out of the passenger doors as fast as we could. We wanted to be out of the hot stuffy car and Nick was anxious to see the inside of a big rig. The cab of the truck was cool and the trucker had an ice chest with soft drinks in it. The trucker walked up to the cab and said,

"I got some Dr. Pepper in bottles in this ice chest. You know, there isn't much Dr. Pepper in California and whenever I travel cross-country I load up on it and keep it cold. I got plenty to last me for a long time, so get you each a bottle and enjoy it".

We both looked at mom, and she shook her head yes so we dug into the cold ice chest and pulled out a dripping wet and ice-cold Dr. Pepper. The drink tasted sweet and spicy and tangy. We sat in the cab of the big rig and listened to the truckers talk on their radios to each other. Nick had a look of satisfaction and mom looked relieved. We had been very fortunate on our trip and the Rambler had performed valiantly during the three thousand plus cross country miles, through storms, grasshoppers, unbelievable heat, and too often bumpy roads. I thought to myself, the Rambler was ready for a vacation of its own and the flat tire was a message that it was tired and needed some TLC, just like we were going to get at CeeCee's, tonight in California.

We could see the trucker in the side mirror as he jacked up the car with his giant jack, took off the flat tire, and rolled the good spare into place. He tightened the bolts, rolled the wheel to check it for tightness, took the jack down, put the flat tire in the rack, brushed off his clothes and headed back to the cab. All together, it took about twenty minutes, just enough time for the three of us to cool off. The big trucker opened the passenger door and Nick and I jumped out. Mom slid over and he helped her out. She tried to pay the trucker, but he shook his head no. I heard him tell mom to stop at the first gas station she came to and get all of her tires checked and the flat fixed before taking off to Los Angeles. He got in his truck and we watched him carefully merge into the traffic, he blew his truck horn as he started up the highway. It was loud and fun to hear. Nick let out a cheer when he heard the horn and we all waved at the big trucker. We never got his name; to us he was always the trucker with the cold, cold Dr. Pepper. Before we merged onto the highway, mom said a prayer of thanks, and soon we were headed for the very next gas station to repair the flat tire.

After we left the gas station, we headed west to San Bernardino on the way to Burbank. Mom had planned ahead and via telephone conversations with CeeCee, she had the trip well documented on the map. Of course, if we got lost, we could always call CeeCee and she would come and rescue us. The palm trees grew thicker and the traffic got heavier. I sat in the back seat and marveled at mom's maneuvering of the Los Angeles freeways. If she was nervous she didn't show it. Just before nightfall, tired but happy, we arrived at CeeCee's house. The first things we did after all the Italian hugs and kisses were to wash our faces and hands and run to the table to eat. After five days on the road it was incredibly wonderful to actually sit at a table to eat.
Nothing can compare to the aroma of a great Italian meal and sitting at the table with family. We had made it to California!

❧

"God gives us dreams

A size too big so that

We can grow into them.

Anonymous

❧

Chapter 3

California

Good food, a clean bed, and a hot bath and family!

CeeCee surrounded us with long Italian hugs and kisses and the excitement of having her family close to her. She eagerly accepted us into her life with an explosion of love that we never expected. Dinner at CeeCee's was even more wonderful than I anticipated. We had spaghetti and meatballs, antipasto, and chocolate chip cookies. My hunger for good food and family were finally satisfied. Also, I knew I could bathe in a clean bathtub and sleep with a stomach full of delicious Italian food and in a clean, fresh bed. No more rusty, stained, and ugly bathrooms and no more uncomfortable nights sleeping on hard, lumpy mattresses.

My body was ready for the change and after dinner I began to unwind and yawn. Nick and mom didn't show signs of sleepiness, like me. Both of them appeared invigorated and ready to talk and make plans. As for me, plans and talking would have to wait, I wanted a bath and a bed, right away. CeeCee saw my yawns. She put her arms around me and led me to the bathroom for a long, luxurious bath. She got my pajamas and slippers and brought them to me. I laid my head back into the bathwater and soaked my entire body. I closed my eyes and held my nose closed with my fingers as I immersed my tired body in the fragrant bathwater. CeeCee giggled when she saw me soaking in the bathwater. My long, dark hair floated around my face and my long legs were bent because I was too tall to fit into the tub.

>She said, "Linda, you have grown so much since I last saw you. Look how tall you are! And, you are just as skinny as me."

Then she bent down and pulled me up out of the water and handed me a big soft towel and with tear-filled eyes pushed the hair out of my eyes and said,

>"Welcome home, little sister."

I don't remember much about that evening because after my bath I immediately dropped into bed and drifted off to sleep as I heard mom and CeeCee softly talking in the kitchen as they washed the dishes. I thought how wonderful it must be for those two to reunite again after such a long time.

Cecelia Amanda Fiore Howland was smart. She was the valedictorian of her high school class. She was head cheerleader and president of the Latin Club and debating team. On her own, she applied for and received an academic scholarship to UCLA in Westwood, California.

> "I have to get out of this small town," she whispered to me one night before she left New Jersey.

CeeCee had hazel eyes and was five feet seven inches tall and 127 pounds. Every inch of her was determined that her future lay beyond that small New Jersey town. It was hard for us to accept when she left home, mostly for mom. There was such a difference in our ages that I don't really remember bonding with her but she was my bright spot in a strict home. In CeeCee's freshman year at UCLA she met Fred Howland. He was a senior and a native Californian. He was a film major, his dream was to become a film editor and he was bound for Hollywood. They dated for a year and then another year after he graduated. Then he was hired as an apprentice film editor at Warner Brother's Studio. Then he proposed.

He wanted to get married and start a family. Her decision to give up her scholarship and stay home as a wife and mother was a hard decision for her to make. She loved Fred and thought that someday she could pick up where she left off and go back to school and finish her education. They eloped in Las Vegas because Fred had little family to invite to their wedding. His mother was deceased and his father moved to Europe to live and he had no siblings. CeeCee asked dad to fly to California and give her away but he said he couldn't afford it. Their wish to start a family was granted when Freddie Jr. came along the following year and Kerri followed the next year. They bought a three-bedroom home on a sleepy street in Burbank, California, and CeeCee became a stay-at-home mom.

When CeeCee got the call from mom that we were coming out to California she was thrilled and she joyously prepared for our arrival. She found a small-furnished apartment investigated the high school I would be attending and prepared and froze dinners for a week for mom so she didn't have to cook right away.

The next morning after our arrival at CeeCee's, I awoke very early. Due to the three-hour difference in east coast and west coast time I wasn't sure where I was. The sun had been up for just a short while and I heard birds singing outside. I awoke in a strange room with mom sleeping soundly next to me. I slipped out of bed and looked out the window and saw the mountains in the distance and I thought to myself, yes, I am really in California. I carefully left the bedroom and quietly closed the bedroom door so I wouldn't wake mom.

As I wandered into the living room, I noticed a very large fireplace that took up the whole wall, with two couches facing each other and a large wooden oak coffee table between them. There was an *L* shaped area with a large dining room table and eight chairs. The house was all on one floor and as I walked toward the kitchen I smelled coffee and I heard voices speaking in soft tones. It was CeeCee and her husband Fred. When I walked in, CeeCee got up and gave me another hug and kiss. She asked me if I was hungry, and to my amazement I felt absolutely famished. I nodded and CeeCee smiled and asked me to sit down at the table with Fred as she started breakfast.

I looked around at a very large kitchen, big enough to have a separate counter in the middle of the kitchen floor, which CeeCee called *The Island* and a breakfast area in front of a bay window. She poured me a cup of coffee and I felt very grown up because mom frowned on us kids drinking coffee. But CeeCee didn't treat me like a kid; she treated me as if I were an adult. CeeCee fried sausages and eggs. We ate some delicious bread with a crisp crust, and drank fresh orange juice. We laughed and talked about the experiences of the long trip. Fred said he would clean the car as soon as it was empty and he would take it to have the oil changed and the tires rotated and checked.

"Nick and I will spend the day together and work on the car," he said.

My sister gave him a look of love and appreciation that needed no words. Little Kerri and Freddie Jr. came bounding in from their bedroom, rubbing their sleepy eyes and sat down at the table. I looked at them both and smiled. Freddie Jr. was four years old and Kerri was three.

"Kerri looks exactly like you, CeeCee," I said.

"Yeah, I call her little Xerox," Fred said smiling at his daughter.

"But Freddie looks like Nick!" I exclaimed.

"Yup," Fred said. "Not much of my German genes came through. They didn't have a chance against those strong Italian genes."

CeeCee walked over to her husband and kissed him on the top of his blond head.

"Yes, but he has your blue eyes and those blue eyes made me fall in love with you."

"Really? I thought it was my sparkling personality," Fred said as he grabbed her around her waist and pulled her close. Fred winked playfully at me as mom and Nick came in and joined us for breakfast. In no time, the family all starting talking and the noise reminded me of our loud New Jersey family. My heart ached just a little, but as I looked at the smiles on the faces of everyone at the breakfast table – well, the ache soon disappeared.

> "Now this is more like being home," I said as I started to relax.

Everyone laughed and continued talking and eating. After breakfast, CeeCee said she was anxious to show us the apartment she found for us. That afternoon mom, CeeCee, the kids and I traveled to the new apartment. It was only two miles from her house. It was small, but not too small. There were two separate bedrooms and one full bath. The kitchen had a breakfast nook and the living room had a big window and a small entryway. The hallway had cabinets for linen and such, and the kitchen had a small area for a washer and dryer.

The apartment was on the bottom floor of a two-story apartment complex. There was a pretty garden area in the center that had grass, a walkway, and a few trees. There was a carport for our car, but no garage. The rooms were painted a neutral color and there was carpet in the living room and bedrooms. We had a wall furnace in the hallway and a water heater next to the washer and dryer connections. It was a furnished apartment. Mom looked at the sparse furniture and she had a glazed look in her eyes. She always had her own furniture and this was yet another adjustment for her to make.

As I stood there looking at this apartment, I tried hard to visualize myself living there. My heart was still in New Jersey. The anguish of losing my childhood home and friends and father, in such a short time became real again. I would have to keep this to myself, however, as everyone else seemed so thrilled. The only comfort I could find in this was the plan Maria and I had, to reunite after graduation, but that seemed like a lifetime away.

Slowly, we adapted to our new lives. I wrote to Maria often, about my new school and CeeCee and her family. Maria wrote to me about how lonely she was because I was so far away. Our letters were always full of schemes to fly her out, but we plotted and planned to no avail. We faithfully attended Catholic mass on Sundays at St. Cyrils. Mom went with us. She had her Bible by her bedside and she read it every day. She said she only made it through the divorce by reading and praying daily. Her time in prayer and devotion gave her the comfort and strength to survive the incredible pain she suffered because of the divorce and separation from her family unit in New Jersey.

Mom insisted that we said grace at all meals, even when we ate out. Sometimes, I would feel embarrassed by the prayer. Mom would hold our hands when she said grace; she was a shining example for Nick and I. She put money aside, from the little dad sent to us for food and rent, for us to put in the collection plate at mass. Sometimes our finances were tight, especially before Nick got a steady job and while I was in high school, but mom never faltered. She said it was our duty and our obligation to support the work of the church by giving what we could during Sunday mass.

For mom, the first few years were hard. Every once in while I would see sadness in her eyes. I was sure she was still thinking about dad and her brothers and sisters that she left in New Jersey. Soon mom got a job at a local department store and she grew to love her job selling undergarments at Robinson's. I began to adjust to life in California and CeeCee and I became very close. I had started high school with little enthusiasm. CeeCee helped a lot by taking us to all the local tourist sites. We went to Griffith Park, Hollywood, and to Grauman's Chinese Theatre with all the footprints and handprints of the movie stars imprinted in cement. Fred took us on a tour of Warner Brothers Studio, and of course the beach that we could go to year round thanks to the warm climate of southern California. I was impressed especially with the beaches. Unlike New Jersey they were wide and the sand was warm and soft. I learned to appreciate my Italian skin, because the other kids at school would burn on the beach and I became more golden brown. I still hated my thick curly hair, and being teased about the way I talked! In California everything is *ahh* in New Jersey we said *awe*. The lesson for me was to just listen carefully and practice saying *ahh*.

CeeCee surprised me on my fifteenth birthday and took us all to Disneyland. At last! I wrote all about it to Maria. I wrote about the trams that took us from the parking lot to the front gate. We had a booklet of tickets lettered from A-E that we used to go on the rides. Little Kerri and Freddie were so excited when CeeCee bought them Mickey Mouse hats with ears. They wore them all day. They loved the teacup ride and the merry-go-round and the Peter Pan ride. The Matterhorn was scary but I loved it. I didn't tell my family that my favorite ride was the children's ride called - It's a Small World (I didn't want anyone to think I was childish). I told Maria that I couldn't wait until she comes out and we can go to Disneyland together. Of course, we didn't go to the amusement parks all the time. Mostly, I went to school and helped mom.

From the very first year, I came right home after school and helped cook dinner and occasionally baby sat Kerri and Freddie at CeeCee's. I didn't have a lot of friends and not much of a social life after school. Other girls were going to skating parties and beach parties. As for me, days were filled with doing homework and watching television before going to bed. My overpowering goal was to graduate from high school and get a job and move in with Maria. Sometimes I would be absent from school, pretending I was sick. Mom let me stay home and watch television. I never knew if she thought I was really sick or I just needed time alone. Here we were in beautiful California, in the sunshine and close to the beaches, but sometimes I thought my life seemed to be going nowhere. I didn't have many clothes to choose from because I had little money for clothes, just jeans and blouses and sneakers and a skirt for Sunday mass. I hated school, not because I was different, just because the school was unlike my New Jersey school and I missed sharing my teen years with Maria.

During that time I saw little of Nick because he was busy working and going to college. Nick completed two years of junior college while working part time at a local electronics store. He eventually applied for a job at Lockheed Aircraft. He was accepted as an apprentice draftsman.
I believe our family made the transition from the east coast to the west coast primarily because CeeCee lived here. The first thing CeeCee suggested was that we have family dinners on Sundays. Mom jumped all over this like chocolate on candy! I thought of these dinners as our own California family tradition. It made me

feel like I was back home in New Jersey. It was comforting to me. The Sunday dinners kept our two families linked with a strong bond.

As was the Italian heritage custom, mom insisted on cooking every Sunday meal. Of course, CeeCee occasionally tried to cook a meal to give mom a break. Her offer to help resulted in a short argument between the two. Well, mom always stood firm to CeeCee's original offer that mom could cook Sunday dinners and CeeCee constantly caved in and let mom have her way. Their arguments became routine and Nick and I enjoyed listening to their phone conversations. We would mimic their phone conversations because they were always the same. When mom ended the call, Nick and I chimed in unison,

> "Are you cooking this Sunday? What did CeeCee say?"
>
> Mom would reply, "I told CeeCee, no, no! You cook all week for your family. It is my turn to cook for you and your family. Sunday. I cook on Sundays!"

Mom's decision was final and she always punctuated her statement by pointing her index finger upward toward heaven as if the Lord himself was listening to her. This conversation repeated itself many Saturday evenings and Nick and I never got bored listening to it.

I clearly remember one specific Sunday night dinner at CeeCee's about two years after we moved to California. CeeCee pulled me into the kitchen and whispered,

> "It's mom's birthday next Saturday," she said.
>
> I whispered back, "I know."
>
> CeeCee added, "All she wants is for you and me to take her out to lunch. Are you free next Saturday?"
>
> I groaned, "Sure, where are we taking her?"
>
> CeeCee tried to keep her voice quiet, "She wants to go to Bella's restaurant again."
>
> I moaned this time, "Well, okay. But, CeeCee, you know how she acts in restaurants."
>
> CeeCee let out a little chuckle, "I know, I know. But, it's her birthday. Don't worry, we'll survive." She winked and as she continued, "Have I told you lately how much I love having you as my sister?"
>
> I stammered back with, "Not enough!"

> CeeCee said, "Then it's settled. I'll pick you and mom up on Saturday at noon."

When we walked into the living room mom looked at CeeCee and me with narrowed eyes.

> She said, "Were you two talking about me again?"

> CeeCee said, "No mom, we just finished the dishes. Let's watch Ed Sullivan on TV."

Saturday came much too soon. CeeCee drove to the apartment and picked us up. The dance at Bella's began. Mom's ritualistic demands began with,

> "Don't forget to ask for a table away from the air conditioning vent. You know how cold I get."

As soon as we walked into Bella's, mom stopped a waiter and said,

> "We will need extra napkins at our table. So follow us so you know where we are sitting."

The waiter shook his head and walked away with a shrug of his shoulders. Mom glared at him,

> "Rude, rude, rude. You know these waiters get ruder every time we come to Bella's."

We waited a bit and were escorted to our table away from the air conditioning vent. Mom plopped in her chair and immediately stated with a wave of her hand,

> "I need lemon water. Remember, no ice."

Mom always made her own lemonade at the table to save money! Then she opened her menu, settled back with a loud exhale and said with great emphasis and firmness,

> "Now don't rush me, I want to read the whole menu."

The menus were old and worn and showed the many years of use by customers. All three of us knew that the menu at Bella's hadn't changed. We had been going there for years ever since CeeCee took us there when we first arrived from California. We both sat in silence because we knew that mom read every menu entry and examined them for changes in prices. She wanted to be certain that her girls were not overcharged! Mom was a penny pincher, and she was determined to get the most for every penny spent on lunch. CeeCee and I ordered our usual chopped Italian salad, chopped iceberg lettuce, diced Italian salami and provolone cheese, pepperoncini, black olives, and garbanzo beans tossed with Bella's own Italian dressing and served with two pieces of garlic bread. Mom always ordered a full lunch with soup and salad and an entrée. Her instructions to the waiter were,

> "Put the soup in a to-go container so I can eat it later, but don't put it in until we are leaving so it won't get cold."

CeeCee and I exchanged glances and I knew she was thinking the same thing as I. We were good daughters. No, we were great daughters! We often wished our own daughters would be as good to us as we were to our own mom. We had to pull patience from our bootstraps because lots of patience was needed anytime we took mom to lunch. Mom's rituals were played out just like a scene from a movie. We knew we couldn't order or eat until every ritual was completed, in order and in fullness. We could predict every word, every action, and every gesture that mom would make during her birthday meal. So, we sat in silence and nodded our heads in agreement.

We hoped that the other patrons weren't watching too closely or listening too intently. We didn't dare look around because we were afraid we would notice someone close by whispering or snickering at the three of us. Many years later, I reminisced about these lunches and I thought how silly I was to be embarrassed. This was our mom and even though she could be a bit eccentric, at times, no one else could ever take her place. No one else could remember how we were as babies or how we changed as we grew. Only mom carried those memories with her and only mom loved us as no other person could love us. And, of course, only two daughters who fearlessly endured the birthday lunches and who endured the predicted rituals could continue to love her, abundantly and fully.

Finally, the birthday lunch was served. We knew it still wasn't time to dig in and eat our meal; there was another ritual for mom to perform for her two daughters. The dreaded coffee ritual! It was time for mom to order her coffee. Yes! Right on cue, she requested her coffee, with a flair of her hand as she waved to the waiter. This was the part I enjoyed watching the most. First mom always put a teaspoon or packet of pure sugar into her coffee and two of the little cups of cream. Mom mixed it together with a spoon. Delicately and ladylike she tasted it. Hum, not just right. Mom never, ever failed to add a half-teaspoon of sugar and half of another little cup of cream. Another taste. Hum, not just right. This process continued until the mixture and color was just perfect. Then the unsuspecting, but attentive, waiter topped off her coffee.

> With a frown, she said, "Oh no, I had it just the way I wanted it."

CeeCee and I got to watch the entire process again. After all, how could the waiter know he ruined her perfect cup of coffee? After this, we grasped our hands tightly, while mom said a lengthy grace. Before she started to eat her meal, she insisted each of us girls take a taste of everything on her plate. To onlookers, the two of us probably appeared as toddlers who were being fed by their mother. Mom would offer us the spoon and put it in our mouths and then say,

> "Well now. Wasn't that good?"

We would shake our heads yes, smile, and wait for the next bite. Yes, we could relax and begin the meal. Every eating ritual was finally completed. Now, we had only to endure the bill-paying ritual, our last ritual. When the bill came she would always warn us not to over tip. Mom would lean forward, and in a very confident and loud voice she would say,

> "Girls, don't over tip! The church only asks for ten percent, don't give more than that!"

Again, we nodded our heads in agreement and CeeCee paid the bill without letting mom know what the total was or what amount she chose to tip. As the two of us agreed, what mom didn't know would remain secret with us. Sometimes, I thought mom enjoyed her birthday lunch routine, way too much. I believe it was her way of showing us she was still our mom and was still in control of every situation. Of course, I took two aspirins and dropped into the nearest chair when I got home. The next day, life continued as normal for a teenager bored with high school.

I was seventeen and almost ready to graduate high school. I was a homebody. I loved to cook, clean, iron, shop, and take care of our apartment. I soon planned to get a job and get my own apartment and reunite with Maria. The thought of getting married and settling down with a husband and kids wasn't in my future life plans. Independence was what I wanted and a reunion with Maria, out here, but God had other plans for me.

Halfway through my senior year I received a letter from Maria. She had started working with her mother at the gas company part time and also during the summer months. She wrote me about one of the meter readers that she liked and started to date. This letter announced that she was getting engaged. What a shock! It couldn't be real. Not really! What about our plans and what about me? Even though I was happy for Maria I felt dumped again, that same awful feeling when I learned about dad leaving. Of course, I always knew Maria would get married but I hoped it would be after she left New Jersey. I couldn't imagine Maria becoming a wife. I thought that we were robbed of our teen years together. Now we are going to be robbed of sharing her wedding day! I knew that the cost of an airline ticket to New Jersey was out of the question not to mention I was afraid to fly. It was totally impossible for me to be her maid of honor, something we both planned in detail in our cross-country letters.

It just wasn't fair, not fair at all. Her letter affirmed that our lives were going to take separate paths. I moaned deep inside because the loss was too painful. Maria grew up and I wasn't there to see it happen. One half of our plans and schemes were gone, but still, I was determined to graduate and get an apartment of my own. I could do it! I was a strong, Italian girl soon to become a strong and independent Italian woman. I was capable of getting a job and living on my own. And that was just what I was going to do!

"L" over the heart for Linda.

Chapter 4

John

I instantly fell in love.

During my teen years Nick worked at Lockheed and took night classes at the local college. Nick would come home from work and tell mom and I about his great friends that worked with him. One specific friend he often talked about was a young man who worked across from him at Lockheed Aeronautics.

> "Bring him home" mom would say, " I'll cook him a good Italian dinner."

The thought of Nick bringing a friend to our home for dinner would be awkward. I was seventeen and only had a few friends. I knew I wasn't the most sought after and popular girl at high school. What would I say to Nick's friend? What would I wear?

Mom wouldn't give up about the dinner invitation. She continued to push Nick to bring his friend home to dinner; John was his name. Mom said John needed to eat some of her homemade Italian spaghetti and meatballs. We knew that no one made meatballs as good as mom. Every time mom cooked them Nick would say,

> "Mom these are delicious. You should open your own restaurant and show them how real meatballs taste. We could be rich," he exclaimed!
>
> Mom's standard answer was, "What? Do you want me to stand on my feet all day in a hot sweaty kitchen? No, I cook for my family, that's enough."

With this said, mom would wave her wooden spoon in the air and then bend and kiss Nick on the cheek. Each time she returned to her cooking, renewed and bursting with pride. One morning, at breakfast, Nick shared that John agreed to come to our little apartment for dinner. Yes, mom won again! Mom was ecstatic.

> "When! When! Bring him soon. He needs to enjoy a good meal," she said with a flair of her wooden spoon.

Nick answered that maybe he could bring him this coming Friday evening. I noticed Nick's facial expression became more serious.

> "Well, I need to share something with you two. John is deaf. He can't hear and he

talks with his hands using sign language," he said with a serious tone.

Mom froze. Then she turned and looked at Nick, her face showed her stunned response.

"A young man that can't hear or talk? Well he has to eat, so bring him to dinner. Well, I don't care if he can't hear or talk. If he is your friend he must be a nice young man. Any friend of my son's is welcome in my home, anytime! I will make my meat balls for him and he will enjoy having dinner with us," mom said with a swoosh of her wooden spoon for emphasis.

That evening, before dinner when Nick returned from work, the three of us sat and talked about his friendship with John. Nick told us he learned to communicate with John using American Sign Language (ASL). Nick said that by using their fingers and hands, they form words and phrases. He said this is how deaf people talk and communicate with each other. Their language was spoken through their hands, arms, and fingers and facial expressions.

Through his friendship with John, Nick said he learned many of the common terms and words known as sign language. Mom and I sat mesmerized as we watched Nick while he demonstrated signs for greeting and every-day phrases. I became fascinated with this new language and just couldn't hear enough about this young man called John. This was fresh and exciting to me; there weren't any deaf kids at school and I didn't remember meeting anyone who was deaf. I was interested in learning more about deaf people and how they learned to live in a hearing society. Before I went to bed I looked up the ASL sign language alphabet in our home encyclopedia and started to memorize it. I anxiously waited for the week to pass.

Friday evening came. I rushed home from school excited. Normally I didn't pay much attention to what I wore. But tonight I put some thought into it. I pulled on my blue bell-bottom pants and slipped on my blue van shoes. I picked out a white three-quarter length sleeve blouse that mom had starched and ironed. I put on my favorite long dangling earrings and looked in the mirror.

"Okay." I thought pleased at what I saw. "Now, what do I do with my hair?"

I was cursed with long dark brown thick curly hair with long bangs that covered part of my face. I didn't mind the long bangs so much because I was self-conscious about my too big Italian nose, my thin lips and brown eyes with thick eyebrows and too long eyelashes. Tonight I brushed my hair back into a ponytail, didn't like it and decided to just let it hang loose. I put on some lipstick and then hurried to help mom set the table. When Nick brought John into our apartment, he introduced him to mom and me. He was dressed neatly in kaki pants with a plaid blue and tan shirt and brown penny loafers. I was taken aback by his appearance because he didn't look deaf! Somehow I thought I'd be able to see the deafness.

Dinnertime flew by as everyone tasted and commented that mom's food was the absolute best. John ate and ate. Mom loved giving him a second helping. A young man who respects good food was a compliment for mom. Of course, John didn't speak, but he *signed* through Nick. Mom and I were fascinated by the efficiency of the non-verbal language the two of them shared. We sat there and watched while Nick and John communicated in silence. I watched in utter amazement. It was like watching a symphony being played; although there were no words spoken it was beautiful.

I was totally intrigued; I had never seen anything like it before. John smiled at me many times during the meal. For some reason I couldn't keep my eyes on my food and I returned his smiles. I wanted to take in every gesture and movement he and Nick made to each other as they silently communicated. Right away I noticed that John had amazing blue eyes. They were a clear blue and reminded me of the sky.

Being Italian, blue eyes were a rarity and no one in my family had clear blue eyes; brown eyes with dark lashes were the Italian norm. I noticed that when John signed his eyes and face added to the communication. He would raise his eyebrows when he wanted to make a point. He smiled, a big happy smile when he was pleased. He tilted his head for emphasis, or shrugged his shoulders when in doubt. I discovered that communication was definitely more than words; it involved the entire person.

I instantly fell in love. I knew, at that very moment, that something unusual was happening to me and that my life would be going in a new direction. My outlook on life and on learning turned 180 degrees; from boredom with school to an intense desire to find and absorb as much as I could about ASL, the language of the deaf and John.

John was tall. He was six feet and two inches tall and had strong arms. He had a beautiful smile and of course those blue eyes. I knew that someone as handsome, intelligent, and interesting as he would never, ever find a skinny Italian girl worth a second look. But, I didn't fret over first inclinations. I was too fascinated with his language. Through John, I found an untapped interest in learning something new. I thought I should add the local community library to my after school schedule to search for information about sign language. Each night I drifted off to sleep with excitement and wonder about the possibility of John being part of my future. The next day Nick came home and asked if I would be interested in seeing John again. Nick said John wanted to know if it would be all right if he took me out for ice cream.

> Inside I was shouting, "Are you kidding me?" To Nick I coyly answered, "Okay."

That was the beginning of my lifelong love for John who was my teacher and my hero. John taught me ASL. First he taught me how to fingerspell by spelling out every word meticulously letter by letter. But I was anxious to learn more. Spelling every word took too long and was too tedious. I was impatient! I wanted to learn how to sign words and phrases. I wanted to be able to fully communicate, not just spell words. John's wisdom was once you learn to *sign* you don't want to fingerspell. After three months of fingerspelling, one night on a date on the Santa Monica Pier, I spelled, I-f y-o-u d-o-n-o-t-t-e-a-c-h m-e h-o-w-t-o s-i-g-n-t-h-i-s-w-i-l-l b-e-o-u-r-l-a-s-t-d-a-t-e! He quickly signed *okay*. Finally he taught me how to sign full words.

I learned that a thumb across the cheek was for *girl* and holding on to an imaginary baseball cap for *boy*. He eventually taught me to sign full phrases. I learned quickly. This man and his language intrigued me. We would sign for hours. We shared our childhood, our feelings, our hopes and our fears. I totally loved John and I fully loved his language. It was a language that seemingly had no anger, no judgment, and no small talk. You said what was on your heart and on your mind. I never tired of practicing sign language with John and I improved my skills by practicing with Nick at home. Signing came easy for me, because I loved John and because I wanted to understand everything about him.

I couldn't get my fill. Just think, me the bored teenager scouring the shelves of the local library! As soon as school was over, instead of hanging out with friends and complaining about the mundane life of a teenager, I headed straight for the library shelves where I pulled off book after book. I spent hours reading about sign language. Each time I opened the library doors I knew exactly what section to go to and where to find the answer to my quest. I was so consistent; the local librarian could set her watch by me. She would smile as I opened the door, give me a courtesy wave, and point to my special area of the library.

I learned that ASL was called pidgin and is derived from Indian hand language. I also learned that many years ago, people hid their deaf children or family members because they believed them to be *deaf and dumb*. Deafness was often associated with being mute – someone who couldn't talk. Society believed that because one could not hear or speak, one could not learn;

therefore, one was dumb. It wasn't until 1755 when the French built the very first school for the deaf that society's attitudes about the deaf began to change.

I looked up Gallaudet University, because John had mentioned that he had wanted to go there but he went to a local community college instead to get his AA degree. Gallaudet University, in Washington D.C. founded in 1864 on donated land is the only four-year university for the deaf in the United States. It receives financial support from the Federal government. It conducts extensive research in deafness. All of their college degrees are signed by the sitting President of the United States. Congress passed a law, allowing the university to issue degrees to the deaf under President Abraham Lincoln who was an advocate for the deaf.

John explained there are reasons for specific *signs*. For instance America is a log cabin interlocking and when you signed that, a deaf person knew what it meant. England is an imaginary walking stick clasping hands on top. Improve is measuring (going up your arm) by increments. Coffee is pretending to grind with one hand. Milk is squeezing a cow utter. Morning is sun coming up from horizon. As our relationship and lessons continued, my fascination with John turned to something more intimate. It grew and matured and he became my best friend.

We dated for a year. I longed for our special times together. Since we were in Burbank, we would go to the beach every Saturday. John loved the beach as much as I. I would pack a lunch for both of us or we would buy sandwiches and snacks and spend the day together on the beach. At the beach we were in our own special, silent world. I never took my eyes off him or his gorgeous blue eyes. I didn't want to miss anything he said. Our special times together were fulfilling and exciting. After the first year, I decided it was time for John to meet part of my family – and CeeCee was just perfect!

During our Sunday dinners we often talked about John. One Sunday, CeeCee asked to meet him. I brought him to CeeCee's on a Saturday afternoon. Everyone took to John; he was a natural with the kids. Somehow the language barrier was non-existent between John and the children. Every experience brought new learning and growth for me as a hearing person who signed. I could share anything with John and I didn't worry about someone overhearing our conversation. Our relationship was unique and very precious. As the time passed, John opened his heart to me and we signed more and more affectionately to each other.

I never really thought much about love. Maria and I would read the movie magazines that gave you the fairy tale version and of course the sex part was always there. I thought mom and dad were in love but obviously I was wrong about that. Maybe it had something to do with being Catholic but in my small New Jersey town I knew very few people who were divorced. Almost all the parents of my friends were still together. Once in a while you would hear about a couple getting divorced but it would be in hushed tones or whispered among the adults. I think that's why mom wanted to move to California. No one in her entire Italian family had ever been divorced! And now here I was madly in love with a deaf man; I imagined my New Jersey Italian family would definitely not approve.

John respected my family and me. He taught me to be patient and frugal and said that he would only buy something when he saved for it. No credit cards. John accepted life as it was, grateful for what God had given him. He looked at life with a positive attitude; he saw the half empty glass as half full. He never expected any charity because of his handicap. He worked hard and played just as hard usually at sports or at the beach diving. I knew that even though he was deaf he would always take care of me.

John had a temper, but obviously there was no yelling. Most of his anger was over injustice or prejudice. We both grew up with a love of God and with the values that honesty and openness was the way to an honorable life. But John took it one step higher to a different level of integrity.

I guess it sounds like I am painting him as a saint but you must remember, I am in love!

One night as we sat together on the beach he pulled me close. I could feel the warmth of his strong body and I felt his breath on my face. He tilted his head toward mine and pushed my unruly, dark curly hair from my forehead. I thought, yes, he is going to kiss me right here. How romantic. He put his strong hand under my chin and lifted my eyes toward his. Then he took my hands. My hands began to shake as he took them in his. Then he showed me the *I love you* sign. His eyes were soft and searching my face for approval. I responded that I loved him from the moment I first saw him. Then he signed that he knew he loved me that very first night we shared spaghetti and meatballs in our little kitchen. I put my head on his shoulder and thought, thank goodness for mom's spaghetti and meatballs and for my brother Nick who found this wonderful man for me.

I felt fulfilled and completed because I knew John was my soul mate for life. We kissed and then lay back on the blanket that covered the warm sand and lifted our arms to the sky and signed I love you, over and over at the moon. The silhouette of fingers against the full moon was like a dance between two lovers, free and graceful. During my four years at Burbank High School I had gone out on a few dates. There was lots of hugging and kissing and cuddling. But I was still a virgin. With John, it was different. Maybe because he was older but there was no sexual advances, just cuddling and long kisses. But I was sure that at twenty-five years old John was not a virgin! John taught me about love and how to love, something separate from just sex.

That Saturday evening passed too quickly. Monday, John returned to work at Lockheed and I returned to school. That entire week was one of sheer agony because I wanted to be with John all the time. I couldn't wait until the weekend when John and I could go to the beach, lie on the blanket and conduct our love talk at the moon.

It was time for me to graduate from high school. Graduation came and went and I looked for a job. Within a few weeks I was employed at Prudential Life Insurance as a receptionist. Through all of these changes, I thought it was strange that John and I had never talked about marriage. I decided one night to ask him why.

> He signed, "As much as I love you I cannot ask you to join the deaf world completely."
>
> He continued with a pained look on his face, "I cannot hear music, so there will be no dancing. I cannot talk to you on the phone. Movies would be difficult, because there is no sound for me. I would just be a burden."

I loved this man even more than I imagined. The fact that he wanted to spare me from something I wanted so much was so endearing to me.

> "But John none of that matters to me. Don't you see that?" I gestured.
>
> He signed to me, "Are you sure?"
>
> I signed in return an emphatic, "Yes!"

John took me in his arms and held me close. I thought to myself, this was the reason that I came to California; this was the reason Maria got married and didn't come out. I was supposed to be in John's arms tonight! I felt that there were no barriers to keep us from being together. John gave me his heart that day and his life. My head began to swim with thoughts of a wedding and of course, telling my family about our engagement. I knew Nick would be thrilled to hear the news!

That evening, we broke the news to mom and Nick. Nick was ecstatic and couldn't stop shaking John's hand and patting him on the back.

> He kept saying, "Finally, another man in this house."

Mom's reaction was much different and totally startling. After all, I was in love with John and I knew he was the perfect match for me. I had prepared myself for mom's objection to John not being Catholic. That was a given in my family's Catholic heritage, but I was not prepared for her reaction to John's deafness. The only word I can use to describe my feelings when mom objected to his being deaf was, I was stunned!

My throat began to close and my stomach felt as if it was tied in knots. My face and neck got hot and I became dizzy. I couldn't focus my eyes and then they began to tear. The tears were so heavy that they rolled off my cheek and dropped onto my hands; the hands that John was holding so tightly that I thought my fingers would break. I knew people were talking. I could hear Nick and mom arguing, but I couldn't make sense of the words. Then it happened. My knees began to feel weak and I fell. Nick and John both grabbed me to keep me from landing on the floor. Mom screamed. The next thing I saw was mom wiping my face with a cold, wet towel as she held me in her arms. Then, mom and Nick walked me to my bedroom and put me in bed. Mom turned a small fan on my face as she sat by my bedside and continued to wipe my face with the cold towel. Nick leaned over and gave me a kiss on the forehead and assured me that everything would be all right and that I should relax and sleep. I don't remember John leaving that night.

When I awoke the next morning, the horrible scene of the previous evening began to replay in my head and I started to cry. I knew the engagement would be a shock to mom, but it never occurred to me that John's deafness would be an issue with her. I dearly loved my mom and accepted that she was outspoken. It was certain that mom would continue to defend her opposition to our marriage using good-old fashioned Catholic guilt and fear on me. My mind kept re-playing her words and I began to imagine future arguments with mom. I imagined mom saying things like - He can't hear, you know! This is unchartered waters, are you ready for this? It is a lot of responsibility for you to be marrying a man who can't hear. I could even predict the tone of her voice and her gestures and body language. Until John and I were married, I knew I would be suffering her continual negative verbal digs; this was her way of breaking me down and getting her way. I promised myself, that very morning, that I would not return her verbal jabs and remarks with anger or even a response. I had always been respectful and obedient to mother but this time I would stand firm as I was certain that this was what I should be doing with my life and I couldn't jump in fast enough!

I hurriedly got up and dressed for breakfast. I could hear mom and Nick in the kitchen. Mom was arguing with Nick. I heard ugly comments coming from mom. I waited to go into the kitchen because I overheard mom's quarrelsome voice,

"A deaf son in law! What if my grandchildren are deaf too! How can I talk to them? I can't talk with my hands like you and Linda. I will be left out of the family; I will be a stranger to my own grandchildren!"

As I listened to mom's remarks I began to understand her objection to the marriage. It wasn't that mom didn't like John; mom was looking to the future – her future as the head of our family and her right to be the matriarch of the family. Mom was losing her ultimate familial power and she was feeling threatened. I decided the best defense would be to tell mom that even if my children were deaf, they would always love and respect mom's place as the matriarch of our Italian family. Then I heard Nick respond to mom. I could hear Nick's voice but I couldn't make out what he was saying to mom. I thought why is he whispering? What could he be saying? I strained to hear Nick's response to mom's outburst, but I couldn't make out the words. Then it got really quiet and my mind started a new worry - how was John reacting to last evening.

John did not understand prejudice. There is no word for prejudice in sign language. How could I explain mom's reaction to him? I did not want to hurt John or make him feel unwanted in my family. I wanted John to be part of my family and to be totally accepted by every person. My head began to ache as I worried about things that could possibly happen to ruin my beautiful wedding day. I sat on the bed and I held my head in my hands and moaned. Just then, mom walked into the bedroom. The expression on her face wasn't angry or tense; she looked as if she had been crying. She took my hands from my head and said,

> "Listen to me little Linda, you think you are grown up, but you are still my daughter. I say, if my little Linda finds happiness with this man, John, who cannot talk or hear - then I find happiness for my daughter. But, remember; don't stay away from your mom when you get married. Every Sunday is family day and I cook! My new son-in-law will eat lots of good Italian food! You understand what I am saying to you, Linda? Don't stay away because he is different from us. Yes, I know, I know. I don't always say nice things about other people, and I have a sharp tongue. God convicts me of that. But, we are happy Italian Catholics who love each other, fight with each other, and sit down together on Sunday and bless the Lord and eat together. That's what life is about - being a family and sharing life together. How can I tell this to your husband to be? I don't know how to tell him. I am afraid he will not accept me

> because I can't tell him these things. You know, he may keep you from me, Linda."

Hearing these words was the best medicine for me. My headache flew away and I kissed mom on each cheek and she returned the kisses.

> Mom said, "Someday you will bring me babies to love and rock and feed. That is what I want!"

With these final words, we made our way to breakfast. I could smell the coffee, crisp toast, eggs, and sausage. My stomach pains were replaced with a healthy appetite. As I gulped down the food, Nick gave me a wink of his eye. I knew he had taken care of mom's objections and he had smoothed everything with John. My worries were over, my wedding would be beautiful. Now it was time to plan the wedding and I knew who would help me, CeeCee and Fred! With mom's acceptance and approval, our path was cleared. Over the next weeks, little by little John told me about his childhood and the challenges he faced growing up. Again I was fascinated and humbled by the ease with which he accepted his difference and how he never blamed anyone, not even God. But I will let John tell you his story.

John

Chapter 5

John's Story

My hands became my voice.

I was born in Solano Beach, California. I was the youngest of five children. I was raised with my three sisters and a brother, all who had perfect hearing. I was born deaf, no one knows why. My mother was loving and protective but she didn't know what to do with me. She tied round little bells on my shoes so she could tell where I was. I learned to communicate primitively by pointing and grunting. That seemed to work for my immediate needs.

I don't remember much of my early years except that I thought I was the only deaf person in the world. Then I thought maybe when I grew up I would be like everyone around me. As I looked at their faces, I saw their lips moving and I knew they were trying to communicate. Naturally, I didn't know what talking was or what it sounded like. I just knew I was different, because I didn't know anyone else who was like me, deaf. I remember vaguely that mother and I sometimes took a long train ride to see a doctor who examined my ears. Then she took me to speech therapy to learn to talk. Of course, that was almost futile because I couldn't hear the sounds of talking therefore I couldn't mimic them. I remember being frustrated and ashamed because I was different.

I started school around the age of six but was ill prepared to learn. The teachers let me sit anywhere I wanted or wander around the room. They passed me from grade to grade because they didn't want me in their room another year. The other children sometimes laughed at me and so I responded by making funny faces to entertain them. Somewhere around third grade I remember we got a visit from a nice man, Mr. Garland. He spoke with mother about my deafness. He learned about me from people at my school. At least once each six months he came to our house and talked to mother. He was a retired teacher from the Riverside school for the deaf. Mr. Garland asked mother to send me to his deaf school to learn a new language called American Sign Language (ASL). When he told her it was a boarding school, she refused to give permission for me to leave home. Mr. Garland did not give up! He was determined! Each time he delivered the same message. He was a true advocate for deaf children. Mr. Garland was determined that totally deaf children were deserving of a good education. He knew that without acquiring good communication skills I was doomed to a life of disappointment. At the middle of my fifth grade year, he came again.

"Please, just go with me to visit the school," he pleaded with mother.

Mother must have agreed because one cold windy December day he drove his Buick LeSabre to our house. All three of us rode in his car to the school. My life was forever changed for the better. Once at the school, mother's eyes were filled with the beautiful sight of many students communicating at a rapid pace with their hands. She saw the light in the eyes of the boys and girls. The teachers at the school took time to assure mother that John was fully capable of communicating using the same skills as the students at the school. Even though mother experienced the miracle of deaf kids talking and learning that day, she was still reluctant to give permission for me to leave home and board at the school. Eventually, mother gave in and her decision became the pivotal life-changing event for me – I would soon be able to talk with my hands and be able to communicate my thoughts and ideas!

Once at the school, I was given tests to measure my hearing loss, to measure what I already knew, and to decide the appropriate grade level for me to start school. My first round of tests showed that I was performing at second-grade level. Within three years, I was up to par and fully participating at the same grade level as kids that hear. I cannot explain the joy, relief, excitement, and pride I felt every time I was able to *talk* to the other students.

Mr. Garland watched over my progress and he introduced me to sports. I joined the basketball and football teams. I realized I could do anything any other kid could do, except I could not hear. I had a roommate, Matt. He was my buddy because we did everything together. It was a tremendous relief to have a close friend, someone to hang out with who was a normal, energetic, curious kid, just like me. My school days were not a lot different than any other kid's but my weekends were often filled with the old frustrations.

I went home to see my family each weekend and holidays. I tried to share with my family how happy I was at school and I wanted to tell them about my activities and the new things I learned. The downside of going home was that no one at home understood the language of the deaf; they didn't know ASL. They wrote notes, but that was tedious and time consuming. I wanted to talk to my family and share with them my enthusiasm about my school. Eventually my brother learned ASL but he didn't stay home very long because he joined the Merchant Marines. My sisters married and were busy raising their own families and mother and father didn't show an interest in my new language.

I tried to explain to my parents how isolated I felt when I was home and that I didn't grow when I came home. I actually regressed and this made me feel like a real loser.

Matt, my buddy and best friend, often invited me to his home for weekends. He said his parents both knew American Sign Language. I thought this was the perfect solution, instead of going to my home I could go to Matt's home and continue to improve my sign language skills. It took a lot of persuading but eventually mother and father agreed to an alternating schedule between Matt's family and my home for weekends. This schedule continued until I graduated from high school.

Just being around hearing people who signed really improved my ability to communicate with the hearing world. Those weekend visits were a true blessing and my signing continued to improve. Time passed quickly and I graduated from high school. Mr. Garland tried to enroll me in Gallaudet University in Washington D.C. but my grades were not good enough. I was accepted at another college, Riverside City College. I enrolled as a freshman at Riverside City College in the deaf program with many of my friends. I graduated with my Associate of Arts Degree in drafting.

With Mr. Garlands help, I discovered that Lockheed Aircraft in Burbank, California had a unique program designed to employ the deaf. It didn't take me long to decide to apply at Lockheed! My roommate Matt also applied and when we were hired we rented an apartment in Burbank. Many of our deaf friends lived in the Burbank area that made the move easier.

What a perfect life for me, hanging out with my deaf colleagues and working for Lockheed. I was also part of a deaf basketball team and we played against teams that could hear. Since we couldn't hear the whistles of the officials, we used special signals to alert each other when there were fouls or the time clock was stopped. I was lucky. My life turned around because I was blessed to have a guardian angel, Mr. Garland.

Then my life took yet another turn. Across the drafting table from me was a young man called Nick. He wanted to become friends and asked me to help him learn ASL. He was a good student, and little by little we were able to sign quite freely. Then he asked me to come to his house for dinner and I met his sister Linda.

**Charlie who kept
my secrets.**

Chapter 6

Our New Life

My sister - my best friend.

Since we relocated to Burbank I had time to build a close bond with CeeCee, my older sister. We became more than sisters, we became best friends. We often called each other and talked for hours over the phone. When possible, we spent time together shopping, cooking, and of course, babysitting her two adorable children. It was natural for me to go to CeeCee first about planning the wedding. CeeCee and Fred were delighted that John was going to join our family. They even learned a few signs, so they could communicate with John so he wouldn't feel left out of family conversations.

This turned out to be a positive decision that helped my deaf husband make the transition more easily into my hearing family. John never shared his apprehensions with me of joining a fully hearing in-law environment. I was so naive and so much in love that I never gave one thought to how he might fit into our boisterous family. Now I think back over those years, I feel that I could have done more to help John prepare for his new world compiled of hearing, talking, yelling, arguing, laughing, loving, and joking relatives. John loved it all. Of course, my brother, Nick was a huge help during this time because he knew sign language so well.

Life in our west coast Italian family continued and now our family was planning a wedding for John and me. CeeCee and Fred were tuned into the future wedding. We all decided it was time to work on the details. When it came to getting married, John and I had mixed emotions. We talked about God and our strong belief in Jesus and a commitment of service to others. But where would we get married? John didn't want to get married in the Catholic Church and I knew my mother would be dreadfully unhappy at us if we got married in John's Episcopal church. I called CeeCee, my only hope to find a solution.

> "Oh CeeCee! What am I going to do? I can't seem to make everyone happy," I cried.

> She immediately came up with a solution, "Have it at my house, get a justice of the peace to marry you here. We can decorate the house, mom can make lasagna, and the family will be together. John's friends can come you'll see it will be fun. Don't worry about mom, leave her to me," she exclaimed in her confident voice!

Truly, I love my sister who is my best friend! With CeeCee's help, my wedding day jitters began to settle down. CeeCee and I found my dress in a bridal shop in Burbank on the rack for eighty dollars; a great deal that went well with my small budget. It was white velveteen with long sleeves. It was lined to the floor, with white daisies stitched around the bodice and down the long satin train. It was a winter wedding. John proved to be a great problem solve, too. He had a friend who was an ordained Christian minister who was perfect to perform the ceremony. He was deaf and was able to perform the ceremony using the language that John, Nick, and I all understood and loved ASL. Nick was John's best man and interpreted the ceremony for the hearing. CeeCee was my matron of honor. I remember that I was blissfully happy at my *silent* wedding. I was nineteen years old and John was twenty-six years old, we were totally in love.

All of John's deaf community friends came to our wedding and were signing to each other during the ceremony. The *hearing* part of the family, John's parents and sisters and my mom and CeeCee's family all sat on one side of the room staring and not talking. It was a quiet wedding; there was no music, no dancing just mom's homemade lasagna. My wedding day was peaceful, loving, and just perfect thanks to CeeCee, Fred, and Nick.

As John's bride and now wife, he not only opened the world of the deaf for me, but he gave me a special sign for my name. John's name for me was an *L* over his heart, a forefinger straight up and thumb to the side to form an *L*. The position of John's hand over his heart clearly indicated that *L* (Linda) was his wife and his love. To better understand the language of the deaf, I must explain how individual names are given.

Names are very personal and always describe the person's physical characteristics or their personality. For instance John's friend Manny was an *M,* three fingers folded over the thumb from the shoulder to the opposite hip because he was six feet and four inches tall and weighed two-hundred and sixty pounds; he was tall and large. His wife Alice is an *A* over the cheek because she had dimples. Janet was a *J* on the corner of the mouth for her big smile. CeeCee was a *C* twice on the jawbone. These special sign names, traditionally come from a deaf person and it is an honor to receive one.

It is a part of the deaf culture to give each other these names. Every day I discovered more about sign language. I learned that it was best to look into the person's eyes while signing. The deaf person you signed to had to watch your hands as well as the expression on your face to fully grasp the meaning of the message. John and I discovered that our conversations in a hearing crowd could be very intimate because we could sign private things to each other and no one would know what we were saying. We could be across the room from each other and sign *I love you* and we didn't worry about someone over hearing.

During the first months of our marriage, we started spending more time with John's friends and I became split between the *hearing* world and the deaf world. I was getting so good at signing with John and his friends that most people thought I was deaf, too. I never felt alone or deprived of my previous hearing world. I was totally comfortable with my new environment. The more I learned about John and his deaf world the more I knew I was in the right place and that God had placed me there for a purpose. I learned that John was a lesson in humility. He never questioned his deafness nor did he ever blame anyone for his difference. He never felt sorry for himself. He knew that not being able to hear was not vital to living or learning, and it was not essential for success. He embraced his deaf culture and knew better than anyone that the only thing he couldn't do was hear.

Our home after we married was a one-bedroom guesthouse behind the owner's home on a tree-lined street in Burbank. It was small and cozy. John surprised me one day and brought home a dog, a small yellow Labrador puppy full of energy and love. We named him Charlie. John taught Charlie how to protect me. When John and I wrestled in front of Charlie, he would growl and show his teeth at John. I learned there was a second reason John brought Charlie home, John taught Charlie to be his ears. Charlie learned to alert John when the phone rang or someone knocked at the door. Charlie became part of our family.

Soon after our wedding, I quit my job and stayed home and became a housewife, a position I loved with all my heart. Sometimes John had to work away from home and I would be alone for a few nights. Charlie slept on the bottom of our bed and stayed by my side as I went about my housewife duties during the day. Charlie was my protector when John wasn't home and I always felt safe with Charlie. During the weekdays when John worked, Charlie and I spent the day together, cleaning the house, marketing and romping at the park. Charlie had a special place in the kitchen where he sat and watched while I cooked dinner, wishing for a morsel of food to fall to the floor so he could gobble it up. Charlie was a true companion to both of us.

During those first years, I discovered a creative side that I cultivated. With very little money I used my creative skills to fix up our home. I painted walls, made wreaths out of dried twigs and leaves, wallpapered with brown paper bags that I had burned the edges of and glued on with a glaze. I strung eucalyptus seeds to form a screen for a doorway for atmosphere. I decorated with candles and made potpourri. John marveled every night when he came home at the changes I made each day.

> *"It's like I come to a different home every night,"* he signed to me.

I was in love and happy just being a wife. We discussed starting a family and John and I decided to wait a year before having children. John was afraid they would be deaf and I was praying that they would be deaf. I loved my husband so much and I also loved being part of his world; I enjoyed his friends and the many fun times with them. Deaf people have a wonderful sense of humor and are able to look at life with a positive point of view. I believe it is because they don't hear the negative tones in our voices.

John's deaf friends were many. This didn't surprise me; other people were drawn to John just as I was. There were probably fifty people who could say they were his friends. There were always picnics and parties and sports events that kept us busy. We were particularly close to John's roommate from school, Matt and his wife Carol, and their two young daughters. They lived a few miles from our house and stopped by to visit on a regular basis. No invitation was needed to visit us because all of his friends became our friends in a very short time.

In the summer the men played softball at the local park followed by a potluck picnic. One specific day in June, I was at the picnic table alone putting out my macaroni salad and cold cuts from the Italian store. I turned to see a young girl who was about seventeen years old. She walked up to me with her hands on her hips. Her stance and face glared defiance and anger toward me. I was shocked and couldn't speak when first seeing her. It was so out of place to see someone in the deaf community show anger or hostility. I looked carefully at the young girl but I didn't recognize her. I meekly signed hello to her and that I didn't think we had met, yet. Her steely eyes never left mine.

> "I'm Emma, Eden's daughter. I have a question to ask you! Why did you marry a deaf man? Weren't there enough hearing men for you? Why don't you leave the deaf men alone?" She signed her defiant question.

She signed all of this in a flurry of gestures and fingers. I was shocked and a little angry. Was this the ranting of a silly, jealous teenage girl who may have had a teenage crush on John? Or, was this something other deaf women questioned? It never occurred to me that our marriage could be an issue or that there would be feelings of resentment toward me.

Yet, in all reality, here was this young, angry girl challenging me and I had to face the truth of her questions. I felt my throat close as if I were choking.

> Then with resolve I signed, *I love him and he loves me. It's that simple, and nothing more.*

She turned her back to me, straightened her shoulders and stomped away like a soldier. If I hadn't been so shocked and unprepared for her attack, I think I would have laughed at her comical exit. Immediately, Carol came over and put her arm around my shoulders and patted me lovingly. I think I was shaking all over because Carol hugged me tightly as if to stop the shaking. Carol saw the whole conversation. I responded to her hug and began to slowly calm down. I worried, was this an isolated incident or was it a message warning me to stay away? Carol explained that there were a limited number of eligible deaf men. Women were resentful when the men married outside of their deaf culture. I told John about the incident on the way home. He didn't say much.

> He nodded his head and gave me a kiss and signed, *you handled it well.*

"Take the time to

Polish up the Golden Rule

And use it!"

Anonymous

Mom's tools for Sunday dinners!

Chapter 7

Mom

The dreaded test!

By now, mom was solidly settled as matriarch of our Burbank family. Her full name was Yolanda Theresa Pilone Fiore. She was born in the central part of Italy in a small town called Penne. She traveled across the ocean on the ship *Stampalia* to America with her mother Marianne and brother Tony in 1914. I can remember growing up hearing the stories about life in Italy, the exciting ship crossing and early life in New Jersey. Mom was raised in a strict Italian Catholic community. A community that was filled with old traditions, guilt, fear, and prejudice; all four mixed together for good measure. Matriarchs of Italian families expect respect and honor from everyone, especially their own children. Even grandmother chimed in with her reprimands to us children.

When I was ten years old my maternal grandmother died. For the last six months of her life she lived with us. She was born and raised in Italy and didn't speak one word of English.

Mom was her translator. Although, everyone believed my grandmother understood a lot more than she let on. On occasion I would come home from school and pout that the kids at school were being mean to me. I would cry that the teachers and friends at school (never, never, Maria, though) were just awful to me. Grandmother would overhear me and ask mom to translate. Grandmother would turn her head and tilt her face downwards with her still black eyebrows pressed upward, she gave me her all knowing and all powerful look. Us kids called it *the look!* With the tips of her fingers together to form a triangle she would shake them at me and say in Italian, "What's the matter with you? Don't you know anything? Little Linda you have to be nice to people before they can be nice to you! So, Linda – start being nice and you will see people return the favor to you!" I learned that this statement was grandmother's version of the *Golden Rule.* Today, as an adult, I can still visualize grandmother and hear her voice chastising me for complaining about something that my own behavior had caused. Grandmother's chastising didn't stop when she died; my mother managed to hand down to me many of grandmother's cautions.

Although I dearly loved mom and respected her old-fashioned traditions I often had to bite my tongue or giggle to myself when outrageous things came out of her mouth. She constantly told me to

> "Pull the shades down, the man across the street will see you," or "You're a wife now, you shouldn't smile at other men."

Mom called me every night after John and I got married and I am sure my sister CeeCee received the same telephone calls. One night the phone rang at the usual time, 7:30 p.m., mom's voice was her normal authoritative tone,

> "I was wondering when you were going to call me?" She asked.

Conversations with mom never started with a normal greeting such as hello or how are you.

> "But mom I just talked to you last night," I replied to defend myself.

Mom didn't waste words; she got right to the point,

> "Never mind, no excuses. I have something important to tell you," she announced with her normal authoritative voice.

> "Okay," I said waiting for the sky to fall in on me.

> "Did you know that your sister is doing yoga?" She said.

> "CeeCee," was my wimpy reply.

> "Yes!" She yelled back! "Well I don't like it! Did you know that they light candles and chant? It's not right, she's gonna go to hell, I'm telling you!" Another yelled response!

Mom's voice was almost at a screaming shrill by now.

> "But mom, I hear it's wonderful exercise for the body and the mind and there really is nothing religious about it," I tried to answer calmly so she wouldn't hear the pain in my voice.

Mom's voice raised another decibel and I moved the telephone farther from my ear.

> "Might have known you'd stick up for your sister." Then, mom said, "I'll talk to you tomorrow," her usual response followed with a click as mom abruptly hung up the phone.

> "Goodbye," I said to an empty phone.

As I hung up the look on my face told John whom I had talked to. He looked at me with his kind and understanding face.

"Your mom?" He signed as he gave me a comforting smile.

"It's not funny, you don't have to hear her!" I signed back with emphasis on the word hear.

"You must keep a sense of humor Linda or she will get you every time. What did she say?" He signed.

I told him and he started to laugh and then he walked to me and kissed me gently.

"If she weren't your mom you would see the humor in all of this," he signed.

I responded by rolling my eyes and letting out a sigh of irritation. John easily read my body language and he knew I was really upset. He leaned down and hugged me with his big strong arms and my sigh of irritation turned to a sigh of relief. Oh John, I really do love you, I thought. John loved my mom because she was a part of my family and me. He would never say anything bad about her, but he tried to protect me from the pain of some of her verbal attacks.

"Well. I guess so," I signed to respond to John's question.

Then, I heard a knock at the door. It was Nick. Our dog, Charlie, also heard Nick and he barked and ran to the door. Seeing Charlie bound to the door, John looked up as I opened the door for Nick. John happily walked toward Nick and the two men met with their usual greeting as Charlie watched with his tail wagging his whole body. My brother Nick enjoyed hanging out with John. He was a frequent visitor and often came unannounced. Nick and John watched football, basketball, baseball games, and sports that were televised. Sometimes, on weekends, Nick and John went water skiing. Since Nick still lived at home with mom, he used these visits to get a break from mom. Two days later, about 2:00 p.m., I received a call from CeeCee,

"Hey little sis," she loved to remind me that I was her little sister.

"How are the kids?" I asked.

"They miss you. Come over more often. I don't like to gossip, but Fred and I were at the Smoke House Restaurant tonight and we ran into Nick and his girlfriend," she said with an air of authority.

"What girlfriend?" I asked. "Tell me more," I prodded.

"Well she is very pretty, and they seemed to like each other a lot," she added.

"Does mom know?" I asked.

"He asked me not to tell her yet," she said.

"Do you think she will pass *The Test?*" I asked.

CeeCee's voice caught, "Oh, no. I forgot about *The Test.* Well, she is on her own on that one."

We talked about the dreaded *Test.* We witnessed it more than once, and mom was an expert at administering *The Test* on a moments notice. *The Test* was what mom did when she first met any girl that Nick brought home, or a girl he brought to Sunday dinners. Mom used *The Test* for the distinct purpose of informing the girl that no one was good enough for her son. She would ask the girl some very personal questions that were absolutely improper, especially when first being introduced. Mom asked her to describe her family background such as, what religion she embraced. If not Catholic mom pursed her lips, lifted her eyebrows, and gave Nick a disapproving look. The next series of questions centered on her ability to cook; specifically what Italian dishes she cooked, how many children she wanted, and how did she feel about spending every Sunday with the family. After several girls refused to continue to date Nick after *The Test,* he stopped bringing them home to meet mom. A wise decision that certainly increased Nick's ability to retain girlfriends.

"Are you and John coming over for Easter?" CeeCee asked.

"Where else would we go?" I answered.

"Just once I would like to be able to cook for a holiday in my own house in my own kitchen!" CeeCee exclaimed!

"Not in our lifetime, or should I say mom's lifetime," I said.

"Yeah, I guess your right," CeeCee sighed.

"Mom brought me over more moppeens today," she continued, "I already have two drawers and a linen closet full of them."

Moppeens were dishtowels in Abruzzi talk. Mom used them instead of aprons. She tied them around her waist and wiped her hands on them while she cooked. I don't know where she found them. They were large white cotton cloths that were very absorbent.

"You don't have enough?" I asked.

CeeCee said, "If I complained, mom would give me that *look* and say, 'You can't have enough moppeens!'"

I chuckled, "She brings them over to me too, I have two boxes of them in the garage. She means well."

"I know, I know. Got to go and pick up the kids from school. Love ya' more than a bubble bath," was CeeCee's closing to our conversation.

"Love ya' more than a hot fudge sundae," I said in response and hung up the phone.

Easter was just around the corner and it was a particularly interesting family holiday. On Easter Sunday morning mom arrived very early at CeeCee's. Mom busied herself as she prepared the traditional Italian Easter soup or Zuppa Di Pasqua and leg of lamb, roasted potatoes, hard-boiled eggs, and salad. Easter was the only holiday we did not serve Italian pasta. The eggs were always hard boiled and colored by Kerri and Freddie Jr. the night before. CeeCee made sure they were displayed beautifully in a basket so everyone could admire how beautifully the kids decorated them.

That year, mom was particularly anxious and nervous on Easter Sunday. She always insisted everyone sit down at least ten minutes before she served. Of course we knew her intention was to hear her family pronounce their ultimate satisfaction with the food. We always praised her with several oohs and aahs and mom's face glowed as she walked around the table placing each dish very carefully onto the table. When the food was finally served we paused for a prayer of thanksgiving and mom insisted everyone clasp hands. After John and I were married, he became part of our Sunday meals. Since John was deaf, and our prayer was always spoken, I chose to interpret the prayer for him.

John and I couldn't hold hands and bow our heads because I needed my hands free to interpret the prayer for him. This became a new opportunity for mom to cause a scene by insisting John and I hold hands. I gave my explanation to mom. Mom refused to accept my explanation from the first year and for all the remaining years we gathered as family for every holiday dinner. It was frustrating for me but John took it all in with his usual calm attitude. He always gave me a smile and never, ever responded to mom's objections. What mom didn't know was that when she bowed her head and closed her eyes, we would drop one hand and I would interpret the prayer for John. After that Easter Sunday dinner, CeeCee and I washed the dishes, while John, Nick and Fred watched sports on the television. The kids played board games while mom, thoroughly exhausted and thoroughly pleased with her culinary creations, napped in a chair. Her work was done.
Two days later our phone rang, like clockwork at seven-thirty pm.

I quickly picked it up and said, "Hi mom."

"How did you know it was me?" She asked. I ignored the question.

"What are we having for dinner Sunday?" I asked.

"Your favorite," she quickly replied.

"But mom, everything you make is my favorite," I said trying to stave off any impending outburst of objection from mom.

"Yes, but this is really your favorite," she said.

"Eggplant parmesan?" I asked.

"No," she said; I could tell from the tone of her voice she was getting impatient with me.

"Beans and Escarole?" Another wimpy response from me.

"No! No! Steak Pizziola," she answered.

"Mmmm, I do love that," I gushed. She immediately changed the subject.

"Listen! My car is making funny noises. Can John check it out this weekend?" She asked.

I thought, okay, this is the real reason for her call. I signed her question to John, who signed back to me, *yes*. I always thought the sign for *yes*, which is a closed fist, moving forward and backward, looked like a bobble head doll. Mom had complete confidence in asking John to work on her car. He never ceased to amaze me. He could fix anything! His curiosity for learning never seemed to stop. He learned how to tune-up a car by touching the engine block to feel the smoothness of the engine. John had a great sense of humor. He often teased me and signed to me, *I tuned it by ear*. He kept moms car running like a top and always washed it for her.

Tell her Friday after work, or Saturday, he signed to me.

"Well, it's six and a half of one, or a dozen of the other, I'll take Saturday," she said.

I started to correct her by telling her it was six of one or a half-dozen of the other, but she had already hung up. I hung up the phone and sighed in relief. I truly love that woman, I reminded myself. If nothing else mom kept our lives interesting by constantly surprising us.

Sometimes she would make an unannounced visit. I remember one specific Saturday mom showed up at the door with a stranger. He was in his thirties. Mom excitedly blurted out,

> "I brought a deaf man home for John to meet!" She exclaimed!
>
> I stood there frozen in my tracks. "Uh," was my only reply to mom. *Hi,* I signed to the stranger.
>
> "He's deaf. Quick go get John so they can meet, they must have lots in common. He's deaf, too," she repeated, this time a little louder.

John's face made an expression I had never seen. He signed to me,

> *She brought home a guy for me to meet because he is deaf?* He asked.
>
> I shrugged and signed, *yes they are sitting in the living room.*

Mom did surprising things like this on occasion. She would pass John in her car and beep the horn at him and say, "Hi John." Then she would shake her head and mumble to herself, "I don't know why I do that, I forget he can't hear." John was polite to the stranger and we all chatted a bit. This stranger was named Paul, he was passing through town on his way to hike in the Sierras and after about a half an hour he excused himself and left. Mom had found him in the grocery store. He was from Idaho and we never crossed paths with him again, or should I say, mom never did! We were married almost a year when one evening, mom rang the doorbell, another surprise visit from mom. She showed up with a paper in her hand and an anxious look on her face.

> "I want to talk to John, you interpret for me!" She demanded!
>
> "Okay mom, come in," as I motioned for John to join us.
>
> She said, "John, I want to apologize," as she put her flat hand on her chest. "When Linda wanted to marry you, I said no. I was afraid, afraid of what I didn't know. But I was wrong. You have been so good to my Linda and me. I love you like my own son. Last night I woke up and God gave me this poem for you."

Her voice started to crack with emotion as she began to read her poem.

To My Son In Law

A son-in-law is once removed, from being one's own son.

I know that by the man made law, that's exactly how it's done.

But slowly as the years passed by, I reasoned with my loving Lord,

How many thoughtful things you do!

The helping hand, love and respect, all inside me neatly stored,

I see a kind and caring heart, a man of strength in many ways.

My prayers go up for you with all the ones I love, most every night and sometimes days.

And now, I'd like, if you'll permit, to change the law around a bit.

Because you fill a special place inside my heart, in no small space,

I've chosen you to be the one, from this day on to be my son.

There was a pause when she finished. The pause gave us a chance to compose ourselves and let the words absorb into our hearts and minds. John got up went over to mom and sat next to her on the couch and cradled her in his arms as they both cried. From that day on, they were both each other's champions and my heart was full.

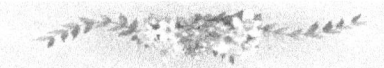

From our family to your family. Cut out the recipe and enjoy with family and friends!

ZUPPA DI PASQUA

1-quart chicken stock
1-teaspoon olive oil
1-small onion, sliced thin
6-eggs whisked together
1-head of escarole washed
Salt and pepper to taste
Grated Romano cheese

Sauté onion lightly in olive oil. Add chicken stock and cook over low heat for 10 minutes. In separate pot place washed escarole leaves and 1 cup water and boil until tender for about 10 minutes. Remove the leaves, drain and chop into small pieces. Add leaves to stock. Add salt and pepper.

When ready to serve add beaten eggs and cook gently until eggs become fluffy and are cooked through. Serve immediately with grated cheese.

Chapter 8

A Chance Encounter

A new friend and a new experience.

John and I enjoyed our grocery shopping trips together. We shopped every Saturday at the local Alpha Beta Market. Every week we got the same reactions from people as we went up and down the aisles with our shopping list, rapidly conversing with each other using our sign language. Sometimes people were so shocked by us they stopped and stared as if they had seen aliens from outer space. Others backed away as if we carried a terrible contagious disease. Of course, there were always the over friendly shoppers that smiled and patted us on the shoulders as if to show their sympathy for us.

It used to embarrass me that people could not accept someone who was *different* and that would somehow make me feel uncomfortable but not John. He just took it in stride and smiled politely. There again I had to realize that John could not comprehend the prejudice of the hearing world, but it would infuriate me. When I would tell him how I felt, he would smile with those kind blue eyes and sign *not worth it*.

One day, John and I were standing in the check out line at the grocery store and as I usually did, I was signing to John and speaking to the cashier. When we started to walk away, the gentleman who was standing behind us in the line tapped me on the shoulder.

> "Miss, I couldn't help noticing that you are hearing, yet you sign very well," he stated.
>
> I turned to face him and replied, "Yes."
>
> "Excuse me for intruding, but if you have a minute I have an unusual request of you," he said.

I looked at John and signed what the man said. We pushed the cart to one side and leaned on the cart while the man introduced himself.

> "My name is Brian LaRue," he said.

He took out his business card and handed it to me and I handed it to John. He continued,

> "Dr. Brian La Rue, I am a psychologist, and your name is?" He asked.
>
> "My name is Linda Miller and this is my husband, John," I replied.

John and Dr. Brian La Rue shook hands. Dr. La Rue continued,

> "I have a private practice. But on Wednesdays I volunteer at the Haven for Hope Halfway House in Van Nuys. Three weeks ago a young girl came in. I believe she is between eighteen to twenty years old. I can't tell you her name at this time due to confidentiality issues. She is deaf and frightened. I desperately need an interpreter to work with me. I can't successfully communicate with her. My ability to help her is seriously hindered. I have asked for an interpreter, but the facility cannot find one. When I saw you today and you are so close to her age, well, I thought you might be willing to help me. I wonder - would you be willing to donate one hour a week to interpret? It's possible there may even be some pay involved."

I was feverishly signing to John when Dr. Brian La Rue stopped. Finally he said,

> "Think about it. Talk it over with John and give me a call. My number is on the card," he said to me.

With that, he shook John's hand again because mine were still flying, telling John all that Dr. Brian La Rue had said and with a nod to me he walked away. John and I looked at each other, puzzled. We didn't communicate on the way to the car, we were trying to absorb all that was said so that we could figure out what to do.

When we arrived home, we started to discuss our encounter with Dr. Brian La Rue. We were so intrigued by his request that we signed late into the night. At first, I was hesitant to make a decision. I doubted my ability to sign to anyone other than John and his friends.

> I signed to John; *do you think I know enough sign language? Should I get involved?*

In the end, my wonderful, loving, caring husband signed to me exactly what I thought he would.

> *"Go ahead it's your chance to help someone.* Then with a playful wink, *I taught you well. You will do fine.*

Just knowing that John had complete confidence in me was all I needed. The next day I called Dr. La Rue and told him I would do it. He was thrilled I accepted his offer to act as an interpreter for a young deaf girl. He asked that I arrive early and that I address him as Dr. Brian and not Dr. La Rue, he thought it was too formal and stiff. He said we needed to meet at least a half hour or so before he meets with the patient. He planned to brief me about the young girl's background and go over confidentiality requirements. He told me I would not be able to share anything that went on in our sessions, not even with John. This would be hard for me as John and I shared everything and had no secrets. Never having worked for a psychologist I was not aware of how important total confidentiality was for the counseling and psychological fields. I told John that night that I would have to keep Dr. Brian's work strictly confidential. As usual he understood. I, on the other hand, was nervous. This seemed like a huge responsibility. I began to worry that I had made the wrong decision and I asked myself, what was I getting myself into?

Chapter 9

Molly

Hidden letters, broken heart.

I left at 9:30 a.m. on a Wednesday morning and Charlie gave me his usual sad look. Charlie and I were always together; we took walks, naps, cleaned the house, and read together. I looked down at Charlie, gave him a big hug and said,

> "Sorry. I cannot take you this time. When I get back I promise we will go on a long walk to the park so you can chase the pigeons."

I don't know if Charlie understood the words I spoke, but he wagged his tail in agreement, turned and walked to his bed, crossed his front paws, and lay his head on them. What a great friend I had in Charlie! He didn't object. I knew he would wait patiently for me to return and that he would greet me with a wagging tail and lots of licks.

When I arrived at Haven for Hope Halfway house, I told the receptionist I was there to see Dr. Brian. In just a few minutes, Dr. Brian was standing at the desk of the receptionist. The receptionist handed him a nametag and he asked me to wear it. Visitor was written on the nametag. He informed me that all visitors must sign in and sign out and return the visitor nametag to the receptionist when leaving. Then we walked to his office.

As I entered his office, I noticed that there was a desk and three comfortable armchairs and a small couch. His desk was empty except for one manila folder on top. I didn't see any personal photos of family or children, and then I remembered that he only volunteered at Haven for Hope on Wednesdays. His phone was covered with buttons and lights and some of the buttons blinked on occasion, but the phone never rang during our conversation. Dr. Brian asked me to sit in one of the old chairs facing his desk.

> Dr. Brian smiled and said, "I want to thank you, Linda. It's a kind thing you have chosen to do. I knew when I saw you signing to John, that you had a heart for this."

I nodded and looked across at this man, seemingly for the first time. I noticed he had black wavy hair, soft caring brown eyes; a kind smile and he wore a wedding ring. He asked if I wanted a cup of coffee or a glass of water or juice. I told him I was just fine for the moment.

He sat behind his desk and I noticed he left his office door slightly ajar.

> He saw my glance at the door and said, "I always keep the door slightly ajar when I interview a female. Since you are not a patient, the best protocol is to keep the door slightly open. I hope you don't mind. Please tell me about yourself. I am very interested in hearing about how you learned to sign so well."
>
> "John. It was John, he taught me," I answered.

I told Dr. Brian everything from the day I met John to the day I met Dr. Brian in the store. I finally paused almost out of breath.

> Dr. Brian leaned forward and said, "Well, Linda. I see you can talk as fast as you can sign, and you are remarkably skilled at both."
>
> I giggled and said, "I sign and talk simultaneously all the time now, and signing is very much a part of my life."

He opened the file in front of him and began to read from it. He explained that the information we were about to discuss was confidential.

> I responded with, "I understand."

The patient's name is Molly. Her brother, Miles, brought her to Haven for Hope. After a year of searching for her, he finally found her on the streets of Hollywood Boulevard. She was a hooker and heavy into drugs. She came from a wealthy home in Beverly Hills, her father was a lawyer in Brentwood and her mother was a hospital administrator. Molly was born four years after her brother. When it was determined that Molly was deaf, her parents were devastated and refused to accept the fact that she was not perfect. Molly's parents never accepted her deafness. When her brother left to go to college, Molly ran away from home at age fourteen. Her parents never searched for her, subsequently her parents died two years ago in an automobile accident. Her brother visits daily and is devoted to her and her recovery. She will go to live with him upon the completion of her time at Haven of Hope. Dr. Brian closed her file and paused for a few seconds.

> He looked at me and said, "Linda, I am going to leave for a few minutes and bring Molly in for you to meet her."

I was nervous when Dr. Brian left to get Molly. I didn't know what to expect. I took a deep breath at that moment and I questioned my being there. Dr. Brian brought Molly in and placed her in a chair across the table from both of us and he took a seat next to me. That way she could see both of us while he spoke to her and I could interpret his words to her.

> Dr. Brian started out by introducing me, "This is Linda", he said. "She is going to be helping by interpreting for me."

He then explained that these sessions would be confidential. I had to explain the term confidential and it was a difficult concept for her to grasp. The only thing close to confidential was secret or private. She finally nodded in agreement.

Molly was strikingly beautiful. She was small in height, a little over five feet tall. She was frail and very much underweight. My guess was an unhealthy ninety pounds. Her frightened eyes were large and blue with deep, dark circles underneath. She had small fine features like a porcelain figurine. Her long hair was unkempt and hung down to the middle of her back. It had been bleached white and was beginning to grow out, revealing a softer, golden blonde. She sat pensively on the edge of the chair and she was continually wringing her hands in her lap. I noticed she rocked back and forth as she watched my hands interpret Dr. Brian's words.

I felt an instant connection with her. This first session, Dr. Brian asked a few background questions but the real intent of this meeting had already been accomplished and that was to introduce Molly to me. It was a brief session, not more than twenty minutes. At the end Dr. Brian asked, as he would after each future session, if she had any questions and she shook her head no.

Dr. Brian and I walked Molly to the door. I signed goodbye and she nodded her head as if to say yes. Before I left, Dr. Brian and I talked for just a few minutes. He said that he was delighted to finally be able to communicate with Molly. All the way home my mind was a jumble of thoughts and feelings. I was excited and then I would be pensive and start to worry. I wanted to be able to share everything with John, but I knew I couldn't because I promised Dr. Brian I would follow his instructions about strict patient confidentiality. When John got home, I explained the confidentiality issues with him and he understood completely.

The following Wednesday, at our second meeting, Dr. Brian began asking Molly about her life prior to coming to Haven for Hope. Molly didn't respond. She stared down at her hands and wouldn't communicate.

> I turned to Dr. Brian and said, "I don't think she is as fluent in sign language as I am. Maybe we should ask simple questions that require a yes or no answer."

He ran his fingers through his dark curly hair, sighed and nodded yes. He looked a little embarrassed.

> "How could I be so abrupt and insensitive? Please tell her we will ask simple questions and all she has to answer is yes or no," he said.

I signed the words to Molly and her face began to relax. She looked at me and waited for the questioning to begin. He asked her if she was feeling well today. She said yes. He asked if she was often sick to her stomach such as vomiting. She said yes. He asked if she felt weak or cold most of the time. She said yes. He asked if she was cold now. She said yes. He stood up and walked to a cabinet that I didn't notice was in the room. He took out a hospital blanket and gave it to her. She smiled and draped the blanket over her entire body. Dr. Brian got a puzzled look on his face and he asked if she needed another blanket. She shook her head yes. He gave her a second blanket and again she covered her entire body. Dr. Brian and I looked at each other – I think we discovered the answer to Molly's inability to sit still.

> "Do you think her rocking and shaking is because she is trying to keep warm?" I asked.

> He said, "Please, please. Ask her."

I asked Molly if she was cold most of the time. She shook her head yes. Dr. Brian looked at me; his face was more relaxed now.

> "Well, that answers many questions and gives me important information that I wouldn't have without your help Linda," he said.

Dr. Brian continued to interview her and Molly continued to answer with a yes or no. Soon the hour session was over. After the session ended, he escorted Molly out of the room to the reception desk and he asked me to stay in his office for a short follow up meeting. After our follow up meeting, I went home. Again, I was disappointed because I couldn't share my experience with John.

The following week Dr. Brian briefed me before our usual session with Molly. He shared that during this session he wanted to gather information about her childhood and family. He said he created a list of yes and no questions that may work. Usually his patients talk about their childhood, but under the current circumstances he had to improvise with a unique set of questions. We started the session with the standard routine, blankets for Molly and the usual seating arrangement. Dr. Brian told Molly this session would focus on gathering information about her childhood and growing up. Before he could start the simple yes and no questions, Molly surprised both of us. The floodgates seemed to open and Molly started signing slowly apologizing for her slowness. Molly shared that her first recollection of any communication was with her brother.

Molly signed to us - her mother and father were cold, silent, and did not try to communicate with her or even hug her. She felt isolated from her parents. Fortunately, Molly had her older brother. Molly and Miles created their own language. They played a variety of games every night he was home. First simple games like Candy Land. Later, her brother played word games with her to help with her growing vocabulary and reading. Molly's eyes and entire demeanor lit up as she shared her memories at home with her brother. It was obvious they had a deep and lasting bond.

She continued to share her story with us - when she was five, her brother told her mom and dad that they must send her to sign language class at UCLA. Her parents agreed and sent Molly to the classes. She loved the fact that there were other children like her. During those classes she didn't feel different or alone. She learned quickly. She taught her brother and they replaced their childhood language with ASL. The school asked her parents to learn the language. Molly signed that her mom and dad said no. We could see the sadness in her beautiful eyes when she shared that her parents adamantly refused to learn how to communicate with her; they refused to learn her language.

Abruptly, after a year, her parents removed her from the ASL classes at UCLA and they sent her to public school. The school was filled with hearing children and no deaf children to befriend her. Her parents were still in denial that she had a problem. They insisted that she attend a normal school. There she floundered. Molly emphasized her pain by repeating several times; *new school, no one like me, everyone had ears.* The teachers didn't know what to do with her. Her brother saw her hurt and brought her books home to read. She signed, *I was happy, brother and books.*

At the age of fourteen, her brother came to her and told her he was going away to college. Molly signed to her brother *that she didn't understand – why? I am afraid without you, please stay.* He tried to console her as he held her hand in his.

> He closely looked at her face and signed, "I will write to you every day. I will tell you everything about the college and my friends and you can write me everyday."

Molly could read his lips and her eyes filled with tears. As much as he tried and tried he could not make her understand what was taking him away from her. When the time came for him to go and he said his goodbyes with tears in his eyes, he made the *sign I love you* with his hand and placed it on her heart.

> Molly signed to us, M*y heart hurt bad. I cry. I no sleep. I wait for letters. No letters, no letters.*

Tears began to stream down her face. She put her hands over her eyes as if she were trying to block out something so terrible she couldn't bear to see it. Dr. Brian was stunned and I was so busy interpreting for him that the intensity of her words didn't sink in. I had not fully comprehended what actually was happening. Dr. Brian had a look of deep sorrow on his face and he turned to me and asked me to ask Molly if she wanted to stop now and continue next week. I got up and went over to her and crouched down and touched her shoulder.

> I signed to Molly, *Doctor is asking, do you want to stop today and start again next week?*

Molly looked at me through her tears and nodded yes. Dr. Brian and I walked her out into the waiting room, and to my surprise she reached out, touching my arm and signed, *thank you.* Dr. Brian saw this as a huge break-through in communication with Molly. After Molly left I began to grasp what actually had taken place and what Molly told us. I on the other hand was totally exhausted, both physically and emotionally. This was a significant session for Molly because she was beginning to relive her story for us, and that was the start of her healing process. As for me, my heart started to break for Molly and it opened up a special place just for her. That night, when I went home, I prayed for Molly's healing and for my own healing too.

After her session ended, Dr. Brian and I went back to his office and he let me read a letter from Molly's brother, Miles. He said it was necessary for me to understand and be able to fill in the blanks of Molly's story.

> Dear Dr. Brian La Rue,
>
> When I came home from Harvard for Christmas break I learned from my parents that Molly had been missing for two months without even a missing person's report filed! My rage was indescribable. They could care less about Molly. They were unflappable. I returned to college telling them I would have nothing to do with them until they found Molly. After that I was pretty much on my own, refusing any money from my parents. I survived on my scholarship, loans and grants and three part time jobs. Molly was constantly in my thoughts. Two years later my parents were killed in an auto accident. To my surprise they left

everything to me. With my newfound inheritance I decided to move back to California and complete my last year of law school at UCLA. I sold the house in Beverly Hills and bought a smaller home in Studio City with a room for Molly. I was convinced Molly was still alive and somewhere in the Los Angeles area even though she had been missing for almost four years. I hired a private detective agency to find her.

It was hard. There were no leads and no one had seen her. My only picture of her was when she was thirteen years old. Nine months passed. Then one day the detective got a lead that there was a deaf girl hooker on Hollywood Blvd. Pretending to be a customer, the detective inquired about the deaf girl. The girls were very tight lipped and said she only saw her regulars, but for two hundred they would set him up with the *Deaf Angel*. The detective said that the *Deaf Angel* seemed to fit Molly's description, but the detective wasn't sure. He asked that I go and make the identification myself.

Molly was hardly recognizable. Her hair was bleached white. She was skin and bones and she was drugged out of her mind. But when I looked into those big blue eyes I knew it was my sister. I signed to her that I was her brother. She started to look at me with disbelief. She was really scared. I told her that I wanted her to come with me. I told her she would be safe and I would never leave her again. I knew I had to get her out of there right away or Sam, her pimp, would hide her and I would lose her again. So with the help of the detective waiting outside, threatening Sam if he tried to stop us, we whisked Molly away. That's when I brought her to Haven for Hope.

Please help my sister. She is sick and scared. I hate being away from her while she is at Haven For Hope, but I know I can't get her clean on my own. Please tell her that I love her and I am waiting for her.

Sincerely,

Miles Cavanaugh

I put the letter down and thanked Dr. Brian for sharing the letter. It was an emotional day and I looked forward to going home. Charlie met me at the door as usual, jumping, spinning and yelping at me as he always did when I returned home. It was as if he were trying to tell me everything I had missed while I was gone. In my exhaustion, I lay down with Charlie on the floor and started telling him about Molly and the difficult life she led out on the streets for four years. I laughed in relief as I reminded Charlie, you are a lucky boy to have a home with such love, but you mustn't tell anyone what I am telling you about Molly. Somehow, telling Charlie helped me to release the stress and emotion of this new experience. I think I needed Charlie more than he needed me. That night, the phone rang at seven p.m.

  "Hi, mom." I said.

  The voice on the other end said, "No such luck, it's your big sister." It was CeeCee. I let out a long exhale of relief.

  "Hey, how's Tricks?" I asked.

  "The kids and I are going to Disneyland next Wednesday, do you want to come?" CeeCee asked.

  "Nope, can't go on Wednesday," I said.

I loved my sister and wanted to tell her about Molly but I respected my commitment to confidentiality and I couldn't go on Wednesday.

  "But, it's the happiest place on earth and you'll love it," CeeCee said.

  "I know but when I am with John I am at the happiest place on earth," I said.

> "You are such a love sick puppy since you got married," she laughed.
>
> "I know, but I am happy," I shot back.
>
> "And I am happy for you too sis," CeeCee replied.
>
> "Have a good time. Love yah more than a pedicure," and I hung up and fixed dinner for John.

Wednesday came and it was time for another session. The night before I had tossed in my sleep as I recounted Molly's story. I worried that I wouldn't be able to interpret properly. I wanted to keep my mind on her words, not on her feelings. Soon it was time to test how professional I was as an interpreter. That Wednesday, Molly continued her story as she told us that when she didn't get letters from her brother she decided to search for him.

> She signed to me, *no letters from brother, I look for him. I look and look and no brother. I got lost and I was alone and afraid.*

Although her story thus far was sad, the next part of her story was particularly painful for Molly, Dr. Brian and me. Molly explained that she found herself on the streets of Hollywood. She said she didn't remember how she got there.

The next memory she has is a man named, *Sam* who befriended the lost and bewildered Molly. She remembered him trying to talk to her but she didn't understand him. When he figured out she was deaf, he started writing notes. He told her he would take care of her. He asked what her name was and how old she was and if her parents were looking for her. Molly wrote her honest answers on the paper and Sam smiled at her. She wrote that she was looking for her brother, but she didn't know where to go or where to look. Sam wrote that he would help her find her brother. He wrote that he wanted to give her a special name; he wanted to call her the *Deaf Angel.* Molly liked the name.

At first, Sam was very nice to her. He bought her grown up clothes. She lived with other girls in a house where they ate, slept, watched TV, took showers, and helped each other, just like real sisters. Then Sam wanted her to take pills and the nightmare began.

Molly seemed hesitant to continue her story. She paused for a while took a deep breath and looked at me with the saddest eyes I have ever seen. That was a clue to me that this part of her story would be unbelievably painful. All she knew was that something had happened to her and she was unclear how it all started. She thought these men loved her, because they wanted to touch her. But some of them got rough with her and made her do things she didn't want to share with us.

Molly did share that she didn't remember much about the next few years. They were a blur of pain, darkness, misery, and temporary relief from pills and eventually shooting up heroin. She shared that her overwhelming desire was to die. At this point, Dr. Brian stopped her and asked Molly,

> "How do you feel now? Do you still want to die?" He asked.
>
> She hesitated for a few minutes and signed to me, *No. That was when I had no brother, now I have my brother.*

To date, this was the most emotional session and Molly's face clearly showed her pain. I reached for a box of Kleenex and handed it to Molly. When she composed herself, Dr. Brian asked his usual parting question,

> "Do you have any questions before we end this session?" He asked.
>
> This time, she looked at me and signed, *where did you learn to sign?*

I interpreted that to Dr. Brian with a questioning look on my face. He smiled and gave me a nod to continue.

> "Go ahead and answer her," he said.

> I kept my answer simple; *I met a deaf man. He was a friend of my brother's and I learned his language, fell in love and married him.* I signed to Molly.

Molly smiled. It was good to see her smile, after all we had spent many hours reliving Molly's nightmare as she tried to find her brother, Miles. After the session ended, before I left for home, Dr. Brian confided in me that Molly was so exhausted after each session that she slept all day the next day. Janie, her nurse, told him that she noticed Molly signing in her sleep. Dr. Brian felt that this was a positive milestone because she was using her language again. It poured down rain all the way home. Charlie greeted me with his usual enthusiasm.

> "I'm sorry Charlie, no park again today, it's raining," I said to Charlie.

I sat on the couch, Charlie's favorite spot for both of us, and he bounded up on my lap. He would stare in my face and it would make me laugh and when I did he would lick my face. This was a routine that he established and I loved it.

> "Ok, Charlie, I will tell you what happened today, but remember, you agreed to confidentiality right," I said as Charlie wagged his tail.

Charlie had become quite a good listener and we have become closer since Molly. He listened so intently, cocking his head as if he understood every word. I always rewarded him with a milk bone.

Before long, I realized we were four months into Molly's treatment. At that time, Dr. Brian greeted me as he announced that Molly's brother was going to be at the session. Molly knew her brother was coming. When Molly came in to Dr. Brian's office he sat Molly on the couch beside her brother. To give Molly a good view of me signing, Dr. Brian and I sat in chairs across from them. Molly seemed to be especially happy to see her brother and they hugged and held hands. Dr. Brian wasted no time, he asked the usual questions of Molly. How she was feeling and did she have any immediate needs? Then he got right down to business.

>"Molly, I want you to turn to your brother, and tell him how you feel about him," Molly looked puzzled.

>*What do you mean? S*he signed.

>"I want you to look at your brother and tell him how you feel about him," Dr. Brian said.

>*I love him, s*he signed, not looking at her brother.

"Please, look at him and tell him that," he said with resolve.

Slowly, Molly turned to her brother and signed, *I love you.*

"What else, Molly?" Dr. Brian asked. "What else do you want to say to your brother?" He asked again.

At this point, I had to stand up and move to a place where Molly could see me signing. A look came over her face that I hadn't seen before.

*I angry at you, s*he signed.

Why? Her brother signed.

She signed, *you went away and you promised you write to me!*

Her brother did not respond. He had a pained look on his face as she continued.

You promised, she continued.

Then she did something I had seen many times before. When a deaf person gets angry they spell every word out using great emphasis on each letter.

L-I-A-R, she signed, *L-I-A-R,* again. *You promised, L-I-A-R.*

Now there were tears in her eyes. Her brother took her hands in his and kissed them, knowing that I would translate for him, as both their hands were entwined.

> I signed his response. *I did write, I wrote everyday. I kept my promise.*

When she saw his answer, she put her head on his shoulder and they both broke down in tears. Dr. Brian motioned to me to leave them alone and we both walked out into the hall.

> "How did you know?" I asked Dr. Brian as he closed the door.
>
> "That she was angry at her brother? That was easy," he answered.
>
> "And she was not angry at her parents?" I asked, a little confused.
>
> "No, they were insignificant to her. They played a very small part in her life. Normally you are not angry with people who are not relevant in your life. It's the people that you have relationships with that you bank on. There is an unspoken expectation of love and trust and honesty with all the people you love, your friends, your family and your loved ones. In Molly's case, she only had one, her brother." He paused.

"Go on," I said.

"Molly's brother told me, he found the letters he sent to Molly. After his parents died he went through their house to prepare it for sale and he found them in his mother's desk, unopened. Now, I will ask him to bring them to Molly to read so she can regain her trust in her brother. We have a long way to go with Molly, Linda, but today was a major breakthrough, I couldn't have done it without you, thank you," he said.

Exhausted, I went home and took Charlie to the park. When we got there Charlie was anxious to play catch, it had been awhile. I finally got to sit down on the grass. I hugged Charlie and while he licked my face, I cried. I cried for all the pain in Molly's life. I cried for the cruelty of her parents. I cried for the comforting and loving words Molly was going to read in her brother's letters. Charlie licked my tears and I cried. Charlie didn't like it when I cried. He continued to lick my face, which I never minded, and this time he leaned back and tilted his head up into the air emitting a soft, soulful, low howl that was his tribute to Molly. In all my years, I have never felt the union of animal and human as I did at that moment. After six months of weekly sessions with Molly and Dr. Brian, Molly was able to spend weekends with her brother as the two were finally reunited. The session after her first weekend visit home she excitedly described her room to us. Her brother had decorated her room at his Studio City home in pinks and lavenders.

> She was anxious for me to see it. *Can you come and see it?* She signed to me.

Molly was starting to sign more and more to me and I had to remind her that I was only her interpreter, not her counselor. Her signing was greatly improved since the first day we began. It was easier to communicate with her because she had learned so many more phrases and was eager to improve her vocabulary.

> *I will have to talk it over with Dr. Brian,* I signed back.

Molly smiled and nodded her head to show that she understood. After that session, Dr. Brian and I discussed the possibility of me building a personal relationship with Molly.

> "Why don't you wait until she is discharged full time?" He suggested.

> "Will she still come back for counseling?" I asked.

> "Yes, her brother assured me, she can come as long as needed. We may have to continue the sessions in my private office

in Burbank, will that be a problem for you?" Dr. Brian asked.

"That would be fine, I'm not ready to give up Molly yet." I responded and I thought my hope was that we could become friends.

Dr. Brian was now working on instilling some kind of positive self-esteem, trust and love into her life, because Molly's hurt ran so deep. He began by asking her to keep a daily journal of her thoughts. In another journal she was to write down her dreams of the future.
Eventually, after Molly finished her stay at Haven For Hope and her rehabilitation seemed complete. She went home to live with her brother full time but continued to go to Dr. Brian once a week in Burbank. With Dr. Brian and Miles' approval, I would pick her up at her house in Studio City and drive her to her appointments and afterward, we went to lunch. I loved our Wednesday lunches together. Molly and I finally were able to talk about personal things, you know, girl things. We talked about what kind of food she liked, what colors she liked to wear, and what nail polish she wanted to buy. For the first time Molly was able to go into public and sign because she was comfortable with me.

Dr. Brian felt that it was time for Molly to meet John. He said it would be good to expand Molly's support system and for many reasons,

John was a good choice. He joined us at lunch the following Wednesday. Molly was excited to meet him. I had spoken of him often. They took to each other immediately and started signing like old friends. Molly's circle of friends was limited to her brother and me, so John was a welcome addition.

Do you believe in Destiny? Is destiny Gods will? If I had not met John I would not have been prepared to help Molly. I never questioned why God placed John in my life but I realized that through John God kept giving me more and more gifts.

ଓଃ

Friendship

Lonely is the un-stretched hand of man

Tightlipped and proud

Unclench your fist and smile

A friend awaits you

If you don't pass swiftly by

By Vi Fiore Spencer (mom)
From her book of unpublished poems
1977

ଓଃ

Chapter 10

Heather

Our Sunday dinners became a festival of delicious foods!

One sleepy Sunday afternoon while mom was dozing after a wonderful meal of Italian stew with tomato sauce and peas, Nick confided in CeeCee and me that he was going to ask his girlfriend, Heather to marry him. He wanted to bring her to the very next Sunday dinner. CeeCee and I held our breaths and asked,

"What about the test," we asked in unison.

"Well, that's why I'm telling you this now, I have already prepared Heather for *the test,"* he answered.

CeeCee said, "Nick, good luck telling mom, we're there for you."

The next day, John and I had just finished dinner and John sat down to read the paper when the phone rang.

"Just giving you a heads up you are going to get a call from mom," CeeCee said.

"What's new about that?" I asked.

"Nick is bringing Heather to Sunday dinner. Nick told mom tonight and she is already huffing and puffing," CeeCee warned me.

"Thanks for the warning." I said. "Ciao."

I stomped on the floor. I often got John's attention this way because he could feel the vibrations of the thump. He looked up.

Did you know Nick is bringing a girl to dinner on Sunday? I signed to him.

He shook his head yes. I was about to ask him what he knew about her but the phone rang again.

"Hey sis," it was Nick on the phone.

"I guess you have heard by now that I told mom about Heather and the dinner on Sunday. I just wanted to thank you in advance for helping me by not leaving Heather alone. I know Mom is going to give her the third degree."

"Don't worry. CeeCee and I will run interference. I can't wait to meet her. See you Sunday," and we both hung up.

I barely hung up the phone when it rang again. It was mom.

"Did you hear, Dominick wants to bring a girl to our dinner on Sunday night?" She asked.

"Hi mom." I said into the phone.

"What kind of name is Heather anyway?" She asked.

It wasn't really a question, and I wasn't going to dignify it with an answer.

"What do we know about her?" She continued to drum me with questions.

"Well," I said slowly trying to think of an answer. "We know that Nick likes her enough to bring her around for us to meet her." Realizing she wasn't going to get any support from me, she grunted,

"Hmmph, she better like Gnocchi because I'm not changing the menu."

"Goodbye mom," I said to my usual empty phone.

I signed to John, *Just once I wish she would say goodbye before she hung up.*

He smiled knowingly.

"*Let's go to bed,*" I signed. "*I can't take anymore phone calls.*"

Sunday came and Nick showed up with Heather. We all liked Heather, she was gracious and lovely and easy to be around. She wore a hat that matched her dress. She looked great in the hat; she was stunning. I never thought of Nick as handsome. After all he was just my older brother, nothing special. About five feet eleven inches and of course, skinny! He displayed the same Italian nose like the rest of us, olive skin and a full head of dark brown hair, but Heather, looked at him like he was a movie star. We could clearly see that she adored him!

She was tall five feet and nine inches with auburn hair that fell over her shoulders. She had beautiful green eyes that twinkled when she smiled and a short nose (of all things). She had a great shape and long legs. It was obvious that she and Nick were in love. Heather worked at Lockheed as a secretary. That's how Nick and she met. Her father owned the Ford dealership in Glendale so she drove around in a shiny new red Mustang. She had two brothers who both worked at the family dealership. We enjoyed visiting with Heather as mom prepared to serve our Sunday dinner.

Mom outdid herself that Sunday. The first course was sautéed asparagus and fresh fennel in olive oil and salt and pepper with a little lemon squeezed on top. Then she placed the vegetables on a platter and surrounded them with sliced mortadella with pistachio nuts and provolone cheese. She served this with crusty Italian bread sliced so thin you could hold it up to the light and see through it. Then she served home made Gnocchi with Gorgonzola cheese sauce. She finished the meal with peeled and thinly sliced oranges drizzled with olive oil and salt and pepper and served them on a bed of butter lettuce.

Heather raved about mom's cooking and even asked for seconds and that made mom happy. After dinner Heather willingly engaged mom in conversation asking her about Italy and listening intently to her stories. CeeCee and I hovered wearily waiting to snatch her from mom's grip. We held our breath when mom asked what nationality she was.

> "My family is similar to a mutt dog. We are Irish, English, Scottish, and German. Nothing like your wonderful pure Italian heritage," she smiled sweetly.

CeeCee and I looked at each other, nodded our heads in agreement; yes, Nick really picked a charmer this time and mom was falling for all of it. Heather completely captivated mom. Nick had nothing to worry about. Heather was smart. She knew the way to mom's heart was to praise her food. Soon, Heather became a regular at Sunday mass and Sunday dinners. Each Sunday we all waited to see what type, color, and size of hat Heather would wear. It seemed that she had just the right hat for every outfit she wore. We loved the newness of Heather. After a few weeks of Sunday dinners, well they weren't really Sunday dinners; we ate at two p.m. sharp. Right away, Heather started calling mom *momma*. Heather went right to the top to get family approval; she focused on the family matriarch, mom! We all agreed this was a smart decision by Heather.

> "Momma," she said one Sunday. "You're the best cook in the world. I could never cook as well as you. But I love to bake. Do you think I could bring over dessert next week?" She asked mom.
>
> Mom took the bait. "Sure," she said and patted her on the hand.

That was the beginning of a culinary apex, mom's cooking and Heather's desserts. She made tiramisu, cupcakes infused with lemon cream, apple pie with raisins and chocolate chips;

she even tried Italian pastries, pizzelle cookies and rum cakes, and biscotti. Our family was in food heaven.

CeeCee and her husband Fred were beginning to sign more and more with John. Even the children delighted in talking to John with their fingers. One Sunday night, Fred suggested that we could go to *Silents*. These are what we called old movies that had no sound, just titles cut in between scenes so the audience would know what the actors were thinking and saying. Also, he said, there were plenty of pictures in Hollywood from other countries that had subtitles translated to English. I leaned over and kissed Fred on the cheek and whispered in his ear,

> "I knew there was a good reason my sister, CeeCee, married you."

John and I decided we would become silent movie *buffs*. As often as we could we had silent movie nights. John's deaf friends found out about it and soon we had as many as six couples going to our movie nights. We would always end up going out for ice cream at Carnation and discussing the movie. On one of these nights at Carnation, while we were signing away, I heard a couple across from us at a table ask their waiter to speak to the manager. I noticed they had been watching us; in fact, I had overheard several negative comments. When the manager arrived, the husband complained to him that we were disturbing them and wanted him to ask us to move. The manager looked around to our booth and smiled at us knowingly and replied to the complainer,

> "These people come in every Friday night, they are regulars and have been for quite a while. You are welcome to change your table if you like but I will not ask them to move."

John and our friends were blissfully unaware of the prejudice that I had just witnessed, and I was thankful for that.

John and I often had dinner on a small white wrought iron table on our tiny patio; whenever the weather permitted. We loved eating out on the patio with Charlie lying at our feet. We didn't have much yard but it was enough for Charlie to romp around in. There was a large elm tree that took up most of the yard. I was thankful for the shade of that old tree because we had no air conditioning. Sometimes we would sit out there for hours and sign until dusk.

> *What would be the one sound you would most want to hear?* I asked John one evening.
>
> He thought for just a moment and quickly signed back, *the ocean!*

All his life he loved the ocean. As a boy he lived a block away from the beach and would swim and dive all day. He continued signing,

> *It looks angry sometimes, when the waves come crashing in. And then it calms down and when it is low tide I can snorkel. What does that sound like?* He asked.

I told him to make the *sh* sound, by pressing his teeth together and pushing air outwards and through them. Even though he couldn't hear the sound, I thought he might be able to feel the vibration of the air moving over his lips.

> *That's what it sounds like,* I signed.

He did it and nodded his head in recognition. Then he pointed to the shadow of the elm tree and signed to me,

> *What does that sound like?* He asked.

> *No sound,* I signed. Next he pointed to the sunset and signed, *and that?* It seemed he was full of questions.

> Again, I responded by signing, *No sound. John you must think it is a very noisy world but there are many things that are quiet and peaceful like your deafness.*

John signed, *even when the shadow moves?* I was taken aback by his thoughts and I signed back,

No, no sound. So when you look at a shadow and a sunset we are the same. We hear nothing together.

At that moment I realized our two worlds had meshed. I was able to get inside his head and understand his deafness. I realized that if he had married a deaf girl she would not have been able to describe the hearing world to him. Now I knew why our worlds had collided and my purpose in life was clear to me. We cherished our dinners on the patio, but of course, we never missed a Sunday dinner!

After church everyone went home, changed clothes and went to CeeCee's. Italians always ate their Sunday dinners in the afternoon and snacked for supper. Mom would have been cooking for hours and CeeCee already had the table set. Eating an Italian meal with a large family is an event. The frenzy of eating, talking, laughing, signing, and passing food around the table was what made it so enjoyable. I believe it was just being together that was special. And always, always telling mom how delicious everything was! Mom planned the menu and shopped all week long for the ingredients. Then on Sunday she was the queen and her realm was the kitchen. She not only cooked the food, she infused it with love. She would let the little children in to her kingdom-kitchen so they could *taste*. The anticipation and the wonderful smells from the kitchen made us salivate until we got the call *dinner is served* and we all rushed to sit down.

For Italians, everything revolves around food! Birthdays, anniversaries, graduations, and weddings, you name it we celebrate by eating! At every meal we say grace and we *toast*.
Italians love to *toast*. We raise our glasses, *clink* with everyone at the table and *toast*. Fred was usually first in line to *toast* because he had taken over as the patriarch and head of his household and of our family.

> "To little Freddie starting Kindergarten," *clink!*
>
> "To CeeCee and Fred's anniversary," *clink!*
>
> "To Nicks promotion," *clink!* And always my favorite,
>
> "To family," *clink!*

I thought someday I would write a cookbook and call it, Culinary Celebrations. *Clink!*

Our Sundays together were special; but I never got over the disappointment that mom never learned to sign – I thought maybe because she already had another language, Italian. After all, she could read and write fluent Italian and would correspond with her cousins in Abruzzi, Italy regularly. It always amazed me when she would get a letter from Italy and translate it to English, writing the English equivalent right under the Italian words, and save it for me and CeeCee to read.

One windy and cold March day, at our usual session with Dr. Brian I felt faint and sick to my stomach. I told Dr. Brian that I thought I was coming down with the flu. He looked at me, slowly shaking his head no and smiled broadly.

> "I think not Linda," he said. "I think maybe you are pregnant," he exclaimed as he pointed to my stomach and winked at Molly!
>
> "What?" I asked.
>
> "Take it from me, I have three kids and I know a pregnant woman when I see one," he replied to my stunned response.

Sure enough he was right. I couldn't believe that he was the first one to know before my husband, before CeeCee, my mother, even before me. Everyone was ecstatic, Mom was doting, John was always smiling and touching my stomach. It was never a concern to John or I whether this child would be deaf or not. CeeCee was delighted to have a niece or nephew coming. Even Molly was excited about the baby. The baby was due the first week in October. I noticed on our Sunday dinners that mom was pushing me to eat more and more "you're eating for two now you know," she would say.

One Sunday, late in April, mom made my favorite - bacala with green salad and just olive oil and vinegar dressing. Lots of bread to dip in the red sauce and Heather made cherry tarts. During dinner Nick and Heather announced that they had set the wedding date for their wedding. It was Friday, August 21st at St. Ferdinand Catholic Church. The reception was to follow at the church hall and then he would take Heather to France for three weeks on their honeymoon. This was exciting news and everyone was jabbering happily, but out of the corner of my eye I saw mom pouting. As expected, that night I got a phone call from mom.

> "Who gets married on a Friday night?" She asked.

> "Hello. Mom? Well, it's difficult to get a church hall on Saturdays anymore," I said.

> She went on without stopping to breathe or listen to my answer, "And then he is taking her to France for three weeks. What is she the Queen of England? Dominick

doesn't have that kind of money," she yelled – I could see mom as if she were waiving her wooden spoon for emphasis.

"Well", I answered. "I think Heather's parents are helping out a bit."

"Madonna Mia! That's not the way things were done in my day. What's this world coming to," she exclaimed. And then, "Get some sleep, your gonna need it, after the baby comes your not getting any," as usual there was a click and then the buzz of a disconnected call.

"Goodbye mom," I said to the empty phone.

The days continued to pass by and my stomach grew. CeeCee called me one day to tell me she had decided to take the children to Canada for four weeks in September on location for a picture with Fred. I told her she owed me *big time* because I was going to be left alone with mom to drive me crazy about what I should be doing during pregnancy. Mom's warnings were different every day,

"No sex, while your pregnant", or, "Don't worry about the pain in delivery, you will forget it after a while," or, "If you want a boy you should eat asparagus."

I could tell CeeCee felt bad. She told me, "I'll baby sit until your baby is twenty-one years old," she offered as a bribe. CeeCee knew what I was going through with mom and she assured me by telling me, "Don't worry little sis, I'll be back in plenty of time for your delivery," she answered, as she was about to hang up.

"I'll miss you more than a bacon burger at the burger hut," I answered.

The next months were filled with Nick and Heather's wedding preparations. Their wedding was going to be absolutely wonderful and spectacular. I suppose the fact that her family had money, and they spared no expense, had something to do with the fancy wedding. We were all excited when the day finally came. It was an evening wedding, so the church was decorated with lots of candles, flowers and white bows. The end of each pew was decorated with boughs of fresh greenery and big white, satin bows. Heather tried to keep it simple, but her parent's had other plans. She had her best friend from college, as her maid of honor, a cousin and CeeCee as bride's maids. I declined her offer to be in the wedding as I was six-months pregnant and I thought I was too big to fit into a bride's maid dress.

Nick chose John as his best man, so I was John's interpreter, from the front row. Heather wore a simple, off the shoulder dress. The bodice was beaded with pearls. The dress was tight and accented her tiny waist. The bottom of the dress was a simple satin, softly flowing skirt with pearls on the bottom and continued on the short train. She wore a delicate strand of pearls, that were *borrowed* from her mother and matching earrings given to her by Nick. Her bride's bouquet was made of all white roses with a single blue flower in the middle for something blue. The bridesmaid's dresses were teal blue and picked up the blue flower in Heather's bouquet. It was a beautiful ceremony. Nick and Heather were radiant as bride and groom.

After the wedding, when all the pictures were taken, we gathered at the church hall for the reception. Heather's family hired a special decorator to come in to make it *enchanting*. There were twinkling white lights everywhere, and lace and ribbons hanging from the ceiling. They had a twelve-piece band that played fifty's music and a full buffet of Italian food in honor of Nick. After the reception, John and I drove Nick and Heather to the airport at Los Angeles International Airport (LAX). We waited in line to watch their plane take off. A young man came up to us with a card of the sign language alphabet and tried to give us one and showed us a box with money in it. He was deaf and begging. John's face turned into a scowl and I could see him gritting his teeth. He gently took the young man's elbow and led him off to the side.

I watched as he scolded the young man. I could see what John signed to him,

> "You make the deaf look bad by begging. I am deaf and I work and you can too. Take your cards and get out of here before I get angry with you. You make me ashamed."

I watched with pride. John was proud of what he had accomplished and he did not want this beggar to diminish all that he and many others like him, had accomplished for the deaf community.

Life returned to normal and I got more pregnant. I saw Molly as much as I could and we often shared family news with each other. I remember the time I took Charlie to meet Molly. I soon discovered that Charlie instantly fell in love with Molly, just as I had. Molly immediately warmed to Charlie and he thoroughly enjoyed her hugs. I noticed how he flirted with her with his sad yellow eyes, but as soon as she started to pet his shining-golden coat his tailed started swishing with acceptance and joy.

Molly loved to brag about her brother's new law practice. She was thrilled that it was flourishing. It was just Miles and his secretary. He needed more help with research and someone to help with his smaller cases. He didn't want to work late because Molly was home. His time with her was precious. So, he ran an ad at UCLA Law School. Two weeks into interviewing, a tall, dark haired, young woman came in; Her name was Sara Houghton. Sara had one more year of law school and wanted a part-time position in a small firm, for experience and extra money. *Perfect,* he thought to himself.

> "Excuse me," she said after a few minutes. "I notice that sometimes you sign as you talk."
>
> A bit embarrassed, Miles said, "Sorry, I don't realize I do it. My sister is deaf and I have been spending a lot of time with her lately."
>
> Sara hesitated for a minute and then said very slowly, "That - has to be a very unique coincidence, because my brother is deaf."
>
> "Really!" he said with emphasis.

Sara could tell by his *really* and the intense interest on his face that he wanted her to go on.

> "Yes," she said. "He is at CSU Northridge, studying to be an architect."

Sara signed as she spoke, to show him her signing skills.

"Are your parents deaf?" he asked. She answered, "No. Mom had scarlet fever while she was pregnant and it affected Bo's hearing."

"What is their relationship with him?" Miles pressed on with questions.

Strange question, she thought. "Well, Dad and Bo, bowl every Tuesday night. They both love sports, so they watch TV and they go to lots of games together. Anything UCLA - my dad's alma mater."

"And your mother?" he continued to ask personal questions.

Another strange question she thought, where is the interview heading?

"She is on several boards for deaf schools, and also awareness groups. You name it. She's on it! She is constantly fighting for new opportunities for the deaf," she answered.

She began to feel a bit uneasy about the interview, it seemed this guy was interested in more than just her legal skills.

Molly's brother listened intensely to Sara as he sat back in his chair, closed his eyes and took a long deep breath. He tried to visualize what life for Molly would have been in that supportive environment. He looked at this beautiful girl, across from him, with long brown hair and hazel eyes and the whitest teeth. He decided he wanted her around for a long time, so he hired her!

It wasn't long until Molly shared with me, at one of our Wednesday lunches that Miles and Sara had started dating. Of course, Miles knew the first time he met Sara that she was someone special. Not surprisingly, Sara's mother fully accepted Molly and immediately took Molly under her wing. She had a special telephone installed in Molly's house so that Molly could communicate via telephone – it was a T.T.Y.

Since Sara and her parents all signed, Molly and Miles started having dinner with the Houghton's. Bo, Sara's brother, began taking Molly to silent movies. Molly's world was expanding and she was making such good progress that Dr. Brian cut her sessions to just twice a month. My world seemed to be absolutely perfect, too; little did I know there was danger lurking in my future.

From our family to your family. Cut out the recipe and enjoy with family and friends!

HEATHER'S ALMOND & CRAN-RAISIN BISCOTTI RECIPE

2 cups all-purpose flour
1 1/2 teaspoons baking powder
3/4 cups sugar
2 large eggs
1/2 cup sliced almonds
1/2 cup (one stick) butter, room temperature
1 teaspoon grated lemon zest
2/3 cup cran-raisins
1/4 teaspoon salt
1/4 cup amaretto (optional)
Preheat oven to 350 degrees

Line a heavy large baking sheet with parchment paper. Whisk the flour and baking powder in a medium bowl to blend. Put aside. Using an electric mixer, beat the sugar, butter, lemon zest and salt. In a large bowl to blend. Beat in eggs one at a time. Add the flour mixture and beat just until blended. Stir in the almonds and cran-raisins. Form the dough into a 13 inch by 3 inch wide log on a baking sheet. Bake until light golden about 35 minutes. Cool for 30 minutes.

Lower oven to 300 degrees. Place the log on a cutting board. Using a sharp serrated knife cut the log on a diagonal into 3/4 inch thick slices. Arrange the biscotti (cookies) cut side down on the baking sheet. Bake until pale golden brown about 15 minutes. Turn to the other side and bake 15 more minutes. Cool before serving.

Chapter 11

Turn a Deaf Ear

Unexpected danger!

Every year, John went to the Southern California deaf convention the second Saturday of September. It was a one-day event. This would be my third year joining him. All of our deaf friends looked forward to it. We even told Bo and Molly about it. But according to Dr. Brian Molly wasn't quite ready for large crowds.

It was always held at the Anaheim convention center across from Disneyland. In past years, John and I stayed overnight and went to Disneyland on Sunday with some of our closest friends, but this time I was too pregnant to enjoy the rides and John thought it was too dangerous.

There was always a large hall with all sorts of displays on deaf reading material, toys that you could put your hands into and do signing for children. Deaf schools had a booth as well as a plethora of booths for insurance for the deaf, new technology, and closed captioning. There was also medical information on new breakthroughs regarding surgery and hearing aids. And everywhere there was ASL (American Sign Language) on tee shirts, sweatshirts, baby bibs, you name it - ASL was on it! I made a tee shirt for John to wear that said, *prevent noise pollution - use sign language.* Everyone wanted to know where he bought it. If I hadn't been so very pregnant, I could have gone into the tee shirt business!

There was also a large banquet room with chairs set up to watch guest speakers from all walks of life that had succeeded in life despite their deafness. There were shared stories from anyone that wanted to get up in front of the large group and sign. There were also movies with closed captions.

The day went by quickly and when the last speaker had finished it was past six p.m. There were still about two hundred of us lingering, not ready to leave our friends quite yet. John was on the other side of the large room signing away with his college friends and I was standing next to an open door to get some much-needed fresh air. The door opened to a cement platform and an exterior cement staircase. I was signing to my friend Anna who was anxiously describing her last pregnancy. Ever since I became pregnant other women seemed compelled to describe their own maternity and birth experiences to me. It was like there was a secret *club of memories* of pre-motherhood experiences that had to be told to first time soon-to-be mothers. These stories properly initiated new mothers into the W*hat I had to go through to have a Baby Club*?   She seemed to be going on and on but I was politely smiling and signing back when she paused, which wasn't very often. Suddenly I was aware of two men's voices outside the door as they were coming down the outside staircase.

> "Ha, ha! The governor won't know what hit him! Pow! One shot between the eyes." Exclaimed a unfamiliar voice.
>
> "Yeah. It serves him right, the son-of-a-bitch! Good riddance to him, " a different voice said that sounded very dangerous.

I became instantly alarmed and my sense of hearing was heightened! My ears strained to hear what they would say next. Even though my mind was aware of the chilling threats, I continued to keep my eyes and focus on my friend's detailed description of her birth pain. But the shock of what the strange voices were saying ran through my body like a bolt of lightening. Their voices were deep and resonant and thick with Italian accents. Their tone sent shivers down my spine and I started sweating down the back of my blouse and my knees felt weak and shaky. Suddenly I became aware that the danger moved closer to me. I could feel an evil presence enter the room - they were at the open door, two of them, one older man and a younger man about my age.

"What's this?" the young man asked.

"Oh, it's okay, I checked them out," said the older man. "They are a bunch of dummies who can't hear and can't talk. They make those crazy hand movements that make them look like freaks."

Oh no, dear God, Linda, I said to myself, *turn a deaf ear. Let them think I am deaf. Keep signing. Keep smiling and whatever you do don't utter a word. Don't look their way or they will know you can hear.*

Then the older man pointed at my bulging belly and said, "Look at that, they're gonna' bring another dummy into the world." At that they both made an evil laugh and walked out the door they came in.

My mouth instantly went dry. I knew I couldn't utter a word. I was terrified! Trying to calm myself, I waited until I couldn't hear them anymore to relax. I thought that if they were out of hearing range, then they were gone. But where did they go? Would they be coming back? With that last thought, my friend finally finished her gory birth experience story and had her baby. My friend was totally unaware of the fear I held inside. She informed us that after birthing two girls she finally had a boy that made her husband happy. By this time what I had heard began to sink in. I took a deep breath and said goodbye to Anna and tried to walk away as casually as I could, even though my knees felt wobbly and my hands started to shake.

Suddenly I noticed my feet were hurting, I had been on them all day and they were beginning to swell. My back was aching from carrying the baby so low and I was hot! I was blindly searching for John and digesting what I had just heard! My legs felt like rubber bands and I was getting dizzy. I began to doubt myself and I thought, *was I imagining it or had I just heard a plot to kill the governor?* To say the least, I was frightened, *What if they knew I could hear? Oh! Where was John?* When I finally reached John, I frantically signed with my shaking hands that we had to leave and that I was tired. Then I grabbed his arm to keep me steady on my feet because my head began to swim and I started to lose my balance. John could read me like a book and he knew there was something terribly wrong. He held onto me and then he signed a quick goodbye to our friends. His strong arms kept me steady as he ushered me out to the parking lot.

What's wrong? Are you feeling okay? he signed to me with a worried look on his face.

I'll tell you in the car, I signed back. *You stay here I'll get the car and bring it around.* John signed.

I tightened my grip on his arm and shook my head no. *No. Don't leave me alone; I'll walk to the car even though my feet are burning*, I signed in desperation to stay close to him.

What's wrong, he signed again after he gently helped me into the safety of the car.

Finally, I could tell him what was bottled up inside me and making me feel queasy. I told him everything that I had heard trying to recall every detail. I started trembling when I repeated it remembering the awful sound of their voices. I was afraid that John would not believe me or think that this was just the raving of a hormonal-pregnant wife. But he hugged me and told me to calm down and breathe.

"Should we go to the police?" I signed anxiously.

John put his hand up then he signed, *Hold on a minute, let me think.*

Then he started the car and the sound of the engine began to calm me because I knew we would be going to a safe place.

We are going to see Molly's brother Miles, but first we are going to get you something to eat and calm you down, he signed reassuringly to me.

It was 8:30 p.m. when we rang the doorbell at the Cavanaugh's house. Miles let us in, took one look at my face and said,

> "What's wrong Linda?" He asked.

> I hurriedly answered, "Oh Miles, maybe it's nothing – but," I didn't get to finish my sentence.

He put his finger to his mouth as if to say hush and he ushered us into his den and closed the door. He could tell by our faces that something was terribly wrong. There was no sign of Molly.

> "Now. What is it Linda?" He asked.

I blurted out the story and he listened intensely then he looked at me like he couldn't believe what he just heard.

> "Are you sure? Did you get a good look at them did they get a good look at you?" He asked.

I told him about the remark about bringing another dummy into the world. At that he grimaced and his brow wrinkled. Miles paced in front of his desk for a few minutes with his head down and his arms behind his back.

> "Listen," he finally said when he stopped and looked at us. "I need to make a phone call, just sit tight for a few minutes."
>
> Then he said, "John, don't worry. You did the right thing to come here."

He left the room and returned after what seemed like an eternity but in reality it was only ten minutes.

> "Okay." He said pulling up a chair facing John and me.

Then he signed to both of us.

> *My sources tell me that Governor Talisman is appearing at the Anaheim convention center on Tuesday night for a large charity event. Linda, this confirms your story."*

He started to speak again, just to me,

> "Now Linda, this is very important. You say there was an older man and a younger man. Did they call each other by name?" He asked.

Miles was getting intense with this questioning.

> I thought for a minute, then I answered, "I think the older man called the younger man Enzo."
>
> "Are you sure?" He pressed with more questions.
>
> "I'm pretty sure," I answered. "Why?" I asked.
>
> "Have you ever heard of the Bonnoveto family?" Another question from Miles.

Both John and I shook our heads no.

> Miles filled us in, "They are the west coast Mafia."

He told us that the Bonnoveto family has two sons, a younger boy about thirteen called Angelo, and the oldest son about twenty-four named Vincenzo, after his father. Miles said he goes by Enzo. Also the Lieutenant Governor who stands to take over, should anything happen to the Governor, is linked closely to the Bonnoveto family. So, if the Lieutenant Governor takes over the state, the Mafia will run it.

> "Do you understand any of this?" He asked me.
>
> "Kinda," I replied.

I started to feel hot, closed in and nauseous. My head was spinning and I was tired, oh so tired. I wanted this to go away! I worried, what had I stumbled into-it all sounded so complicated.

What should we do, John signed to Miles and then he signed, *I am scared for Linda.*

Miles paused before he signed back to John, *I can't say that what you heard isn't serious. It sounds like the Governor's life is in danger, or it could be nothing.*

Should we go to the police? John signed to Miles.

Miles pulled his chair closer, and looked us straight in the eyes and signed to both of us,

Give me some time to do some investigation. Let me make some more phone calls. By noon tomorrow I will have more information and then we can go to the police, if you want. But I warn you. From what I have heard about this family we are dealing with, they are dangerous people. Stories are they even have influence with the police. Go home. Try to get some sleep if you can. I'll be at your house by noon tomorrow. Oh, and lets not mention this to Molly for now, agreed?

Then he looked at us with love and compassion in his eyes, almost tearing as he signed to us,

> *Don't worry you two, we will get through this together.*

John and I went home and got in bed, but we didn't get much sleep. We just lay in each other's arms wondering what the future was going to hold for us. I kept thinking, maybe I shouldn't have said anything. Have I put my baby in danger? My whole family! I was so scared I started trembling, but John just held me tighter I closed my eyes and prayed to God, please let this be a dream and we will wake up in the morning and it will all have gone away.

We got up the next morning bleary eyed. It was Sunday. We tried to eat breakfast but neither of us were hungry. We just sat around quietly waiting for noon to come. Miles showed up about 12:30 p.m. and he looked quite disheveled and sleep deprived, even worse than us. A somber looking gentleman in a dark blue suit, a red and blue striped necktie with a black briefcase accompanied Miles. Miles introduced him,

> *"This is FBI agent, Joe Bander,"* Miles signed. John shook his hand and Miles continued,

> *Last night I called a fraternity brother of mine that joined the FBI and told him what you overheard. It turns out the Bonneveto family has been under surveillance by the FBI for quite some time - mostly for their drug trafficking across the border. Governor Talisman is about to sign a bill curtailing that trafficking. Because of that the police have no jurisdiction on this case. Agent Bander is in charge of the investigation in L.A. He wants to ask Linda a few more questions.*

I repeated my story again, straining my brain to remember every detail in that short encounter. I told him about the outside staircase they were coming down when I first heard their voices. I described them as best I could, but I purposely did not look at them so they wouldn't suspect I was hearing, mostly, I remembered their voices. That wasn't much help to agent Bander. Then he reached into his brief case and brought out some pictures for me to look at. I don't know how, it must have been peripheral vision because I did not look directly at them but I identified the older man as *Luigi* something or other. Agent Bander seemed pleased and actually smiled. I guess Luigi worked for the Bonneveto's.

"Now what?" I asked.

They both looked at each other and then faced John and me.

> Agent Bander said, "These are dangerous people and they can identify you. If they find out you are hearing your life will be in grave danger. We have three days to put our plan in place. But right now we need to put you in a safe place until this is over."
>
> "Your sister is in Canada and your brother is on his honeymoon, right?" Miles asked me.

I shook my head in recognition. Things were happening too fast. I wasn't clear as to what he was getting at.

> Miles said to me, "I think I know a safe place for you to stay where no one will find you for a short time. Tell your mother that John is taking you away for a few days for a second honeymoon before the baby comes and she can't call you."
>
> I said, "She will never go for that. Besides it was Sunday and we were supposed to go to Bella's for dinner since everyone else is gone."
>
> "Okay. Okay. Tell her you will call her every night. Molly and I will take Charlie,

and we will take her out to dinner tonight," Miles added.

Agent Bander chimed in, "Now throw some clothes together we are leaving now!"

I motioned for John to go with me to the bedroom and as we packed I filled him in on the plan. I think John picked up most of the plan because he could read their lips. But I wanted to make certain he fully understood why we were leaving in such a rush.

Agent Bander left and Miles took us to Haven for Hope and stashed us in the director's suite of rooms. It was just a bedroom, a bath and a room with a couch and T.V. and there was no kitchen just a small refrigerator. No one was to know we were there except the director and Dr. Brian. John and I were still in a state of shock; we couldn't believe how quickly our lives had turned around in the last twenty-four hours. We felt so alone and helpless. Sunday afternoon and evening John and I tried to keep busy. We watched television. That Monday dragged by slowly. I found an old game of checkers in the closet and I taught John how to play. But mostly we just signed. We shared our love for each other, renewing our vows privately. We agreed that if anything happened we were grateful for the time we already had (we got a little morbid). We passed the time writing down names of boys and girls for our baby. Dr. Brian's daily visits bringing me tacos and burgers for my cravings were a welcome addition to our lonely days.

The hardest thing to accept was that I lied to mom. She wasn't happy about our abrupt departure. She was smart. She knew something was up. She asked a million questions that I had to make up false answers to. My heart ached because she sounded lonely when I called her every night, but I couldn't worry her or expose her to the awful truth.

The days passed slowly and Tuesday seemed particularly long because we knew that was the night of the convention and the governor's speech. We prayed for his safety and for Agent Bander and his team. We took a long nap, played checkers and watched television, again. The day seemed endless. We woke up early on Wednesday anxiously awaiting the arrival of Agent Bander and Miles. At nine a.m. they arrived with coffee and donuts. I took that as a good sign. Immediately agent Bander started talking to us.

> "For your safety and for security reasons I cannot give you a lot of details but suffice to say you saved the Governor's life, Linda. We were successfully able to protect him thanks to your warning. Mr. Luigi has disappeared and I suspect Enzo will be sent away by his father due

to the failed attempt," and then he said nothing but looked over at Miles as he added, "But Linda, you could still be in danger."

Miles interjected. "If Enzo ever sees you and recognizes you as hearing, well you know," he implied.

Then agent Bander chimed in, "We could put you and John under protection if you want."

John looked at me and signed, *whatever you want Linda.*

I thought for a minute it seemed like a difficult decision but it was easy for me. I took a deep breath and stood up. I signed and spoke with great resolve,

"You mean put us somewhere in North Dakota or Wyoming or wherever and we can't contact any of our family?" I asked. Without waiting for an answer I put my hands on my large pregnant belly for a moment and rubbed it and said,

"This baby, whether it be a boy or girl, hearing or deaf will be brought up with Sunday dinners and the love of our family and friends. I will leave our safety in the capable hands of God! Now we have to go. Mom is waiting for us to come home today and she promised to cook dinner for us tonight, I have to clean my house and we have to go get Charlie!" I said with authority and finality.

We gathered up our few belongings and were happy to be going home. On the way home I felt for the first time that I could breathe without fear and dread of what the future held for John and me. I rolled down the window on my side of the car and let the breeze blow on my face – it felt as if all my worry was caught in the breeze and floated away.

John and I never discussed the convention or the following three days with anyone else. Miles and Dr. Brian held our secret for us. When Mom or CeeCee would ask about out three-day, spur-of-the-moment getaway I just smiled sweetly and told them we had a good time. A week later John showed me a small article in the Times on the second page. It read:

SHAKE UP IN THE GOVERNORS OFFICE

A shake up in Governor Talisman's office was announced today that Sal Schiarafa his Lieutenant governor was resigning due to *personal reasons* and he would immediately be appointing his replacement within the next few weeks. The Lieutenant Governors office would not confirm the information and did not provide additional details. No further comment was given.

There was no doubt in my mind that God had a hand in this. I was thoroughly convinced we were under the protective eye of God through the entire event. I have always asked myself, did God put me by the door that day because it was not the governor's destiny to die at the convention center?

My wonderful husband gave me support and guidance. He helped me focus on what was really important, family and our new baby. Thankfully, between all of us, we were able to prevent harm to the governor. There is that fate thing again; twisting its way through my life. If I hadn't been at the convention that day with John and been mistaken for deaf, I would not have overheard the threat to the governor's life. I decided that I was no longer going to question my fate, my destiny, or my future. I was just going to sit back and enjoy life with John and our new baby and continue our Sunday night dinners.

Chapter 12

Splendida Famiglia

Bo suggested that Molly learn to drive; just short trips because she didn't want to get on the freeways yet. Bo said it would give her a feeling of independence and self worth. It was rewarding to watch her progress. Molly and I even found a Gelato place in Burbank that had luscious lemon that brought back memories of Maria and New Jersey. Our conversations at lunch were all about her new art class, and Bo and his family. John would join us regularly at Don's Burger Hut in Burbank and sometimes even CeeCee, too. Gradually Molly integrated with my family, as I had hoped.

Our family expanded and encompassed more than just our original seven when we first came out from New Jersey. The fact of the matter was that my memories from New Jersey dimmed. Maria and I still exchanged letters; but over the years there were fewer letters. She often wrote that she was busy with her twins and that she and her husband, Tom, moved in with her parents on our old block. It seemed that life in that small town was what she wanted. As for me, I realized that our New Jersey family dinners and holidays were replaced one hundred fold in California. Even after the scare at the convention, I knew that my true destiny was in California with John. Of course, there would always be fears and challenges that cropped up in our life. But my life and my family's lives were in God's hands. Whatever He placed in my path I knew I would be protected by God, and by John, and by my family, and by love.

Our life in California centered on our holidays and Sunday dinners. Christmas Eve at CeeCee's was always a special event. This year would be no exception. Her house was decorated with twinkling lights everywhere; her large tree was bulging with Christmas gifts underneath. As usual, Fred made his homemade eggnog. Mom and CeeCee were in the kitchen making linguini and clam sauce, bacala, shrimp scampi, and stuffed calamari - only fish on Christmas Eve! The aroma's from the kitchen wafted throughout the house and filled my nostrils. I took a deep breath and looked around me.

Nick and Heather were setting the table. Fred was opening the wine for dinner. Miles and Sara were sitting on the couch as Charlie enjoyed being petted. Dr. Brian was getting a cup of eggnog for his wife. Molly was signing to Bo and his parents. She was beautiful in a blue dress and a single strand of pearls. She was different than the girl I first saw in Dr. Brian's office.

Five children were running around the house, laughing and making noise and no one seemed to notice. Our two-month old baby girl, Teresa Cecelia, was nestled in her father's arms. She could hear. God blessed me by bringing me three thousand miles, to John, to CeeCee, and to Molly. I ask you, could I possibly be blessed with more?

EPILOGUE

There has been much advancement for the deaf and hard of hearing since the early 1960s when the stage was finally set to perform in their favor. With the onset of closed captioned television and Teletype (TTY.) It was wonderful for the deaf to be able to call each other for the first time and communicate via the TTY. You would type and when finished, type GA which then meant the other person would *go ahead* and was free to now type. Primitive now, but such a welcomed upgrade from, well, nothing!.

The deaf had to depend on hearing friends or family members to go with them to doctors appointments, dentists, meeting at schools, tax appointments and sometimes job interviews to name a few. Many who had no one to interpret for them would bring a pencil and paper and do their best to communicate writing back and forth. Due to the language barrier between English and *signing* this was often a difficult and frustrating experience for all involved.

John and I rode the new wave into *Deaf Awareness* in those years. Auto insurance for the deaf finally became affordable. Health care premiums dropped. Awareness, discriminations, and new legislation - we felt it was a combination of many things.

1964- was the birth of professional interpreting with the Ball State Teachers College Workshop, in Muncie, Indiana. The first sign language class followed.

1965-the first formal education for interpreters at CSUN was followed by the National Technical Institute for the deaf in Rochester, NY in 1966.

1973- only nine years later, Congress passed a law requiring that Interpreters be provided for the deaf and hard of hearing to allow equal access of services. This bill was called The Rehabilitation Act. It was the *Bill of Rights* for people with disabilities or "the handicapped" as they were referred to in the 1970s. In section 504, it stated that from then on, "there was to be no exclusion of participation, they were no longer to be denied the benefit of or be subjected to discrimination under any program or activity receiving Federal financial assistance."

1990- The Americans with Disabilities Act (ADA) passed. This stated that a business with fifteen or more employees must make reasonable accommodations to people with disabilities. For the deaf, this most often means the provision of qualified interpreting.

These are a very small segment of the laws that were passed over the past fifty years.

Others included rights for children to be educated in the least restrictive environment.
Organizations formed. Promoting ongoing training and certification for interpreters to continue to raise the bar for quality in the field of interpreting and simultaneously provide the best interpreting possible for the deaf and hard of hearing.

Unfortunately there are many John and Mollies out there with parents who do not know how to begin to communicate with a deaf child. It can be a huge paradigm shift for families to adjust to. With all the advancements of today, texting, social networking, and videophones, the deaf and hard of hearing people have become much more independent, and much more educated. I look around today and would like to see more corporations open their doors to the deaf like Lockheed Aircraft Corporation did in the 1960s so that there are many opportunities for the deaf after college. We can mandate much but I still see prejudice in our society toward anyone that is *different*.

God's blessings to all of you who are *different* and wonderful!

Linda Fiore Sanders

Visit our Website. We would enjoy reading your remarks about *Turn a Deaf Ear:*

www.turnadeafear.com

Your comments are important to us as we continue the journey of Linda, a true champion of the deaf.

We would enjoy hearing from our deaf readers their own stories. Your stories enrich our lives and help us to always remember the struggles you face each day.

If you are part of an organization, church, or association that promotes and supports members of the deaf community – please feel free to share this information with us.

Linda and I would truly appreciate the opportunity to share our story with you and your friends. Please contact us via our e-mail:

Janet Horger
janhorger@yahoo.com

Author Information

Janet Fiore Horger

Janet Fiore Horger is a first generation American born of Italian immigrant parents. She intertwines in her stories her strong Italian family traditions and rich language. She is a prolific writer and each chapter of *Turn a Deaf Ear* reflects her imagination as she brings new and exciting visions to you of Linda and her family. She assures that every reader will be entertained and will fall in love with her heroes and heroines!

Linda Fiore Sanders

Linda Fiore Sanders, Janet's younger sister, is the model for the Linda in *Turn a Deaf Ear*. Linda provided the foundation for the stories in each chapter and Janet turned them into exciting works of fiction. The two authors worked in harmony to build a short novel that captivates the reader and sends each reader back in time to the 1960s. The 1960s were a time of the commonplace prejudices of people who were thought to be *different*. Linda Fiore Sanders has always rejected these prejudices; she was able to seize true love as a result of her stand against prejudice!

Grasshopper Christian Publishing
Dr. Zelma J. Frankhouser
Author and Speaker

Coming soon by before Christmas 2011
Margarita's Red Dirt of Oklahoma

Margarita's Red Dirt of Oklahoma contains simple stories for parents or grandparents who enjoy reading to their children and grandchildren and the elementary-age student (ages 8-11) will enjoy reading about Margarita Eileen and her love for her Oklahoma home.

The book contains three stories: *Grasshopper in the Window, The Mystery of the Painted Wagon,* and *The Secret in Grandma's Suitcase.* The reader will follow the life of Margarita Eileen as she grows up and starts school. She and her family will eventually experience the terrible or dirty thirties – the great drought that decimated more than two-thirds of America's farmland.

These stories are Christian-based and the reader will share in the struggles and eventual triumphs of the family as they endure many hardships on their Oklahoma farm.

For more information visit:
www.consultant4nonprofits.com
To pre-order your copy, write to:
zelmafrankhouser@yahoo.com

Photograph of Linda and Janet

Taken by:

Linda Mariano, photographer

Sign Language Alphabet

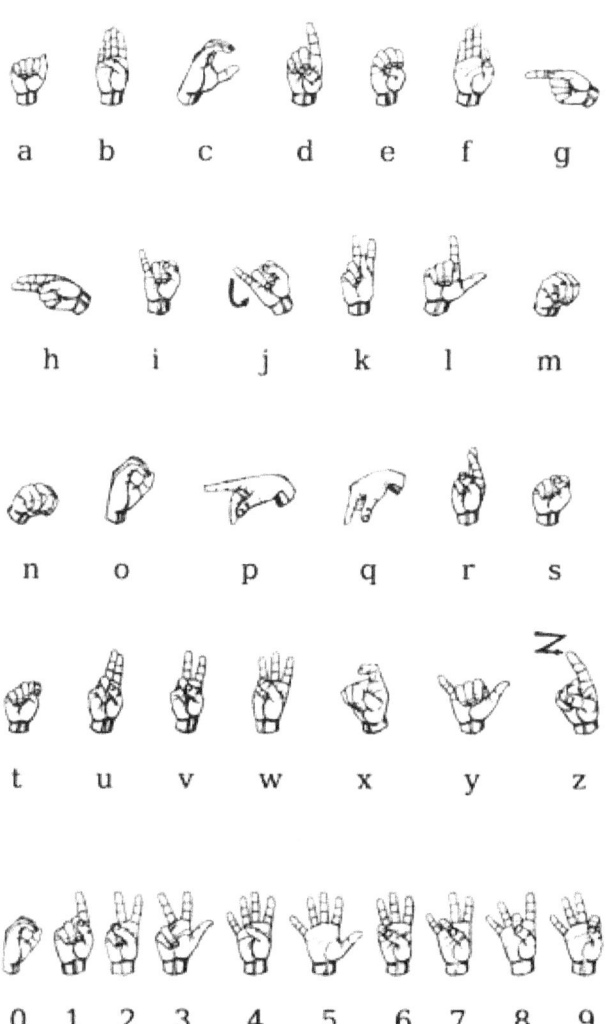

Released into the public domain (by the author).
Gallaudet-TT Font

CPSIA information can be obtained
at www.ICGtesting.com
Printed in the USA
FSHW011958290719
60523FS